THE

SYMBIONT

The Symbiont Time Travel Adventures Series

Book One

———◆———

T.L.B. Wood

Cover and Book design by eBook Prep
www.ebookprep.com

ePublishing Works!
978-1-61417-834-7
February, 2016

DEDICATION

For Lilly Anna

PROLOGUE

The young pup stretched, slowly awakening within the warmth of the den where he lay with his aged mother. Wise one was she, having found this secure location to bear him when she was heavy in her pregnancy. His lupine features stretched in a yawn, and he placed his long muzzle across her flank in a gesture meant both to soothe her and comfort himself. Her life force was waning as she prepared to die. He tried not to concentrate on it, for he needed to stay focused, and grief would overwhelm him, he knew. As his mother took a deep sighing breath, his head jerked up, fearful for a moment, but then she took another breath, and then another. It was not time—yet.

His mother was old, even for one of her species, having seen over nine hundred winters. As they lay there together, he felt her reach out to him with her mind which, despite her infirmity, remained focused and penetrating. She not only knew his thoughts but also could discern his feeling state. He smiled to himself as she told him to not worry. A serious minded one, he could not help but worry a little. Ever since his birth, she had transferred to him her experiences and knowledge—all that he would need to survive in a hostile world—in anticipation of her death. Alone, he would need everything she could pass along just to even the odds he might survive.

As they lay together, she shared memories of a time before his birth. She and other of her species, both beast and the humanoid brothers who were their companions, were gathered around a campfire, sharing the precious warmth. From out of the darkness sprang a group of early humans, intent upon a massacre, fearful of these strange beings—unfamiliar and therefore frightening. The humanoids and canines formed quick parings, and, as they did so, began to vanish from sight. Pop, pop, pop—one after another disappeared, beginning a journey to an uncertain destiny. As the young pup's mother ran towards her humanoid *symbiont*, he turned to protect another member of their party and, in doing so, was clubbed down. She felt his life spark disappear and knew in that moment that her exit from this place was forever closed. In grave danger, she turned and ran. The primitive humans only pursued a short distance before giving up the chase, no match for her speed.

The young male shared her memories of loss and empathetically experienced the intense sorrow; it was as if half of her had died. Shifting his weight, he burrowed his muzzle deeply in the rufous fur of her neck, trying to distract her from her thoughts. It would not be long now, as he felt her life spark slowly extinguish—like a candle was guttering. What would his future hold, he wondered, alone in this primitive world with no companion? Once again, his mother's gentle and familiar mind reached out to his. "Be good," she reminded him. With that, she took a deep last shuddering breath and was gone. He had no tear ducts but inwardly cried for the loss of his mother, his sole companion in an unforgiving world.

CHAPTER 1

The sensation of rushing movement forward had ceased; after a moment, I became aware that I was lying on a hard surface with some object digging painfully into my lower back. I could feel the racing of my heart and lay there, with my eyes closed, until the beats normalized. Finally, I hazarded opening one eye to canvass my surroundings. With gratitude and relief, I recognized the familiar pieces of furniture, books, whatnots and all the other things which came together as a part of my household. The gentle chaos was comforting to me. My slight disorientation, as if I were awakening from a deep dream state, was beginning to dissipate.

I managed to slide my hand beneath my back and remove the offending article on which I lay—one of my old sneakers. I felt, as I always did following a time shift, as if I'd been beaten with a stick... no, make that a forest of sticks. I glanced across the small room and saw a ball of collected dust beneath a chest of drawers, a little dirt tumbleweed I'd missed at some point. Well, I never had laid claim to the title of most meticulous housekeeper on the planet—and felt little remorse.

My little house was comfortably situated on a quiet street, tree lined and old enough to still have sidewalks that were cracked by age and use. Though small, my home would have been the favored dwelling of any number of single people or young couples who were starting out on the brave new adventure of a forged life together. When humans looked at my face, they were comforted to believe that a fellow member of their species gazed back with a clear and honest eye. But I am not human—I am a *symbiont*. And the large creature who lay next to me on the dusty floor was one, too, despite the fact he looked more like a reddish colored wolf with the size and bulk of a mastiff.

I groaned as I sat up, thinking that no hangover on earth quite matched up to the big headed feeling experienced at that moment. As I changed positions, I spied Kipp, lying close nearby. He was still, his back to me, and for a moment, I had a brief dart of anxiety until I saw that his sides were rising evenly as he breathed. Reaching out my hand, I lightly stroked his fur covered shoulder, not wanting to startle him since this was his first experience with time travel. His mind reached out to me, comfortingly, in the easy manner of telepaths.

"Are you okay, Petra?" he asked. His head stirred and he turned to gaze at me with his slanted amber eyes.

"Yes, I think so. How about you?" I asked in return.

He gave the equivalent of a mental head nod.

"Is it always like this?" he asked.

"Well, Kipp, if you feel like you've been down the rapids without a paddle or even a boat, then, yes, you are pretty normal."

Considering his youth and inexperience, I was proud of my new friend. Time shifting was not for the faint of heart and fewer and fewer of our kind even took the challenge. If we weren't by nature such curious little busy bodies, the need to time travel probably would have died off many years ago.

"So, this is your home?" he asked, looking around the room with interest since he had never been inside a modern dwelling—make that any dwelling—before.

I could read his thoughts, of course, and became a little defensive as he started to comment on all the clutter and junk with which I had surrounded myself.

"I admit there is a lot of, well, stuff, here, but I need all these things," I finally said in response.

He widened his eyes and gave me a skeptical gaze. With that, he rose, stretched in a bow, and silently began padding through my small house; I could read his surprise and interest as he wandered from room to room.

"What is this?" he questioned me, his thoughts drifting to me from the rear of the house.

I rose, somewhat shaky in my stance, and wandered back to where he waited. I found him next to a pile of tattered fabric, the remnants of what had once been a wool Hudson Bay blanket. It was tucked in a corner of the small bedroom.

"I smell canine," Kipp observed. "This was Tula's den," he stated.

"Tula could have her choice of anywhere to sleep—she liked this place best of all. She could have stayed in my bed with me, too, but she preferred this old blanket. Tula tended to stretch out and was restless at night." The memory was still painful, and I swallowed hard as I stared at the blanket.

The bond between me and my *symbiont* was the driving force behind the capacity for time travel. Tula— my other half as it were—had been killed during my recent trip to a chosen time in pre-history where I was dispatched to study a tribe of early humans. Kipp, a contemporary of those ancient times, bonded with me in a moment that still seemed to be the product of a miraculous spark of energy. Without him, I would have died, some 70,000 years in the past, a prisoner stuck in time with no way home.

But our choice, Kipp's and mine, had not been without consequences. My group of symbionts would, no doubt, strongly disapprove of my decision to interrupt the natural flow of time in such a manner. Had I changed the future by bringing Kipp home with me? Or should I have lived out my life in a cold cave, waiting for starvation to overcome me?

Kipp continued to shift his gaze around the room. Through the slatted plantation shutters, the late afternoon sun played across the taupe walls, stabbing here and there to illuminate the small space. It was a dark room as I had always preferred it to be, tiny and dimly lit. He walked over to a library table and looked at some of the framed pictures grouped there. One was of me as a young child; he recognized the picture and smiled in his thoughts. He turned to look at me.

"Can we sleep like we did in the cave, lying together with my head on your shoulder?" In his appeal there was a plaintive note, just for a moment—a tiny remnant of the orphaned pup.

"Yes, Kipp, I'd like that, too." My knees were still wobbly and I folded myself into the overstuffed chair that had always been my favorite reading nook. Kipp walked to me in concern, resting his muzzle on my forearm.

"I'm okay," I answered his worried inquiry. "You are younger than I and such travel takes less of a toll on your body."

Kipp's head suddenly jerked back and a moment later I felt it, too. Other *symbionts* were probing us gently, with curiosity towards Kipp and a mixture of welcome and annoyance directed at me. Rapidly following that exchange, Kipp looked at me and his disapprobation of the negative feelings was clearly palpable. Through no great effort on my part, Kipp had become the leading member of the tiny Petra Goodgame fan club. Closing his eyes, he rested his muzzle on my arm again. His ability to concentrate and organize his thoughts, as well as his capacity to marshal, his emotions was amazing to me. His telepathic abilities, from my brief time of observation since our first encounter, appeared to be far superior to any living *symbiont*. His upcoming meeting with the modern version of our kind would be, to say the least, very interesting.

Contemporary *symbionts* lacked the ability of accurate thought transmission over latitudinal distances, and it was but a short moment later that the silence was broken by the ring of the telephone. Kipp gave a start, never having heard such a noise, but rapidly composed himself as he realized I didn't share his alarm. Picking up the phone, I heard the much loved and familiar voice of Philo, my mentor and friend.

"Petra, glad you are home," he said, hesitating a moment before continuing. "We, of course, realize that Tula is absent; we don't recognize the thoughts of the being that is there with you." His voice trailed off, waiting for me to respond.

"Philo, it's a very long story and I'm exhausted," I began, not wanting to be interrogated at that moment.

"But where is Tula?" he persisted.

With a deep sigh of resignation, I answered him, realizing that his question was appropriate and unavoidable. "Tula didn't make it... there was an accident." My voice drifted off. Philo had been very fond of her.

"So how did you get home?" he resumed, his voice subdued.

"That's quite a story and will take time to unravel. I'll tell all at the debriefing; just let me get some rest first, please?"

Even though Philo's curiosity had to be intense, there was really no objection he could mount, so he grudgingly rang off, leaving Kipp and me to our own devices. Finding a can of chopped chicken in the cupboard, I boiled some rice and mixed that concoction for Kipp. For myself, it was something frozen I managed to pry loose from my freezer. It was gratifying to watch Kipp dig into the food, bolting it down with large mouthfuls. At one point, he looked at me, eyes bright and tail waving like a plume, his thoughts transmitting his intense pleasure. I think he enjoyed his meal more so than I did mine. We would have to feed carefully, I had found from past experience—small amounts and frequently for a while.

After we had finished, I stumbled off to the bedroom, exhausted to the core; with little preparation, I fell onto the sheets, forgoing a bath or any other ablutions. My fatigue was intense and complete. Kipp followed me, and after a few moments considering his approach, he carefully climbed on the bed, confused by the soft, malleable surface, and, after some clumsy attempts to turn around and settle himself, he finally lay down, his head on my shoulder. He hadn't wanted to admit it, but he was at the end of his energy stores, too. It was thus we lay for the next 36 hours.

As Kipp drifted off to sleep, his head on my chest and my hand twisted in his fur, I let my mind revisit the time from which I had just traveled and the events which had taken place. I knew I'd have to give exhausting details upon my interview and debriefing and couldn't stop myself, despite my fatigue, from organizing my impressions.

The land was harsh and barren, dangerous and remote. Bands of ancient humans had managed to survive there, carving out an existence by becoming as clever and resourceful as the animals they hunted. But I paid the ultimate price in that I lost my beloved Tula, and, with her death, I also lost the ability to time shift back to my century. Even though ours was a shared risk and responsibility, I knew Tula died trying to protect me, and that thought lingered hard and heavy on my soul. Losing a matched *symbiont* is as profound an event as can occur with our species.

It was fortunate that the group of humans who stumbled upon me, injured and helpless, were as compassionate as they were curious. Even though I differed slightly in appearance, they did not seem to view me as a danger or potentially hostile. Indeed, they were fascinated by me and embraced me to join their small collective. I am slightly embarrassed to say that they viewed me as a good luck charm, a wizard—not exactly a god, but something rather unique.

I was with the tribe of thirty five early humans for about two years, learning their culture, language, and social behavior. That was actually why I had made this journey, what my kind refers to as a time shift. It wasn't for the faint of heart, and many of my species declined the calling, but this exploration of past mysteries was how I made a living. However, I did not anticipate being trapped without a means to return to my century. Being of naturally long life as was usual for one of my species, the two years seemed to pass in a matter of weeks to my perception. During that time, I developed my place in the tribe. The others tended to dote on me, but I stubbornly insisted upon doing my share of work. There was one myth in history that could quickly be dispelled: the men were not just hunters while the women gathered plants, tanned hides and raised the young. The fact was that men and women worked in tandem to bring down large mammals for food. These people were efficient through necessity and used the flesh, fat, bones and every part of the animals they killed.

A mild summer day dawned on the land, which stretched in all directions with low rolling hills to break the vista of green grass and stunted groves of tightly gathered trees. It portended to be a good day for hunting. I tried to linger behind the others as they made preparations to leave the large cave which served as housing for us all. I was not by choice a meat eater but learned to do many things in order to blend into different societies. It would have suited me well to remain at camp while the others engaged in the hunt which, though it might be an unpleasant outing for me, was critical for survival of the people.

Each member of the tribe had a name which was

descriptive and action oriented. This was indicative of
their language structure, which did not consist of words
or letters, but of sounds that encompassed actions and
metaphors. In this instance, as all others, my telepathic
abilities were a plus in terms of decoding and
comprehension. The one I called Leader had early on set
the tone towards me that all others respected and
followed. Finding me in the snow, exhausted, depleted,
and unwilling to leave my dead Tula, Leader gently
pulled me away and, sharing his robe for warmth, helped
bring me to what would be my home. He named me
"She Who Lives with Wolves". Tula was no wolf, but
her appearance was understandably deceptive.

The circumstances, by which I was found, coupled
with my appearance, gave me superstitious value to the
group. So on this hunt, Leader would not be deterred.
Noticing my reticence, he gently took my arm and urged
me to accompany them. It was thus that a party of ten of
our members went in search of giant elk. Tracker, a
young female with preternatural abilities to follow trails
and predict the habits of herd animals, indicated through
gestures that the desired prey was a short distance ahead
of us. Placing her hands on her forehead and splaying
her fingers, she told us that elk were the target. She and
two of the young men, the fastest runners among us,
loped ahead, low to the ground, circling ahead of the
projected path of the elk. Deliberately they put
themselves up wind with a predictable effect: the herd of
elk wheeled back towards our concealed, waiting party.
Leader and his daughter were the most accurate with
spears and waited until the fleeing herd was racing
between two hillocks, our group concealed on either side
of the small pass. Then they struck with deadly
accuracy, taking down two elk with primitive but
purposeful spears. This kill would help sustain the group
for many weeks.

As we moved in to begin dressing the carcasses,
Leader beamed a gap toothed smile in my direction. I

knew his thoughts: my reputation as a good luck charm was sealed and he would want to tote me along on all future hunts. We made a couple of travois sleds and began the long journey back home with our prize. There was much rejoicing at the camp in celebration of the successful hunt.

These people, as I learned, lived a very hard life of toil. They set aside little room for play; the environment was too harsh with many dangers, and they could not afford to let down their guard for a moment. But one day, the group was taking a rare moment of relaxation, lying in a field of tall grass as the sun beamed down to warm and nourish bodies. The freckles which sprang up across my nose in response to the rays were a source of endless fascination and more than one finger gently traced their path on my flesh. Leader engaged in some hyperbolic boasting, telling an unbelievable tale of a time when he had single handedly taken on a pride of cave lions and had emerged triumphant. The others, as was their way, were listening politely, but there were surreptitious mirthful glances passed back and forth among them. As we sat, enjoying the rest and the unusually mild breeze that was caressing our bodies, there was a sudden darkening of the sky, as if a light had been turned off. In concert, there was a shift in the temperature and a cold western breeze accompanied the darkness. Leader jumped to his feet and pointed at the heavens, his attitude clearly fearful at this inexplicable turn of events. Even Flower, the most sensible and calm natured member of the group, had a worried furrow to her brow.

With that, the band needed no urging from Leader to retreat to the perceived safety of the cave. Once inside, they began frantically searching for some comforting context in which to place this inexplicable moment. Of all the members of the tribe, I had grown closest to Flower. She was the healer of the people and had helped treat my wounds when I had first been brought here by

Leader. Possessive of knowledge of plants, information that had been passed down to her healing sect for hundreds of years, she used her talents to benefit all of us. In kind, she instructed her son in this experiential science so that one day he could don her mantle. Most of her days were spent in the low hills, as she constantly searched for roots and various plants that she could put to use in her healing arts. I was always welcomed to accompany her on these little excursions, as I was curious in my role of historian to see her in action.

As the others in the cave buzzed with excitement, she remained quiet, taking her seat close to me. Without using any of their unique language, she reached out and covered my hand with hers. It was a struggle for me to hold back tears. Looking at my friends, I felt a stab of despair, knowing what they did not—either a meteor had struck earth or a volcano had erupted in primitive fury. The subsequent dust cloud that had been kicked up was blocking the sun's light. There would be massive death from starvation to follow.

The people did not have any organized belief system in a deity and they lacked scientific knowledge. But in troubled times, they would turn to the one who was given the task to examine signs in nature and give prophecy. Apparently her grandfather had been considered gifted in this art and the mantle had been passed to her upon his death. Looking back, I think she interpreted signs that might be used today to make pronouncements, such as examining the fuzziness of a caterpillar to predict if it would be a harsh winter or a mild one. Leader approached her with respect and queried her as to her conclusions. As we all watched mesmerized, she appeared to place herself in a deep, meditative state. Not a word was spoken as the people waited patiently for the Seer to acknowledge the room. Finally, she opened her eyes and glanced around the cave, the circuit purposefully slow as her cloudy orbs made contact with each of us individually. What she said cannot be easily translated, but the idea was clear: her grandfather had told her there would be a catastrophic event one day in her lifetime and that the group must leave their home to seek survival. That in itself was sufficient for Leader to confer with the elders and plan to leave what had been our home.

Over the weeks that followed, the small band hovered in the cave, occasionally venturing outside for brief moments. But they were so terrified of the darkness and the changes to the climate, that they avoided going out as much as possible. Even though my species of time travelers was under a strict code of non-interference, if I had known of any way to save these people who had become beloved friends, I would have done so. In many ways, I had already violated the basic tenants of time travel and the cultural observations which were part and parcel of my craft, in that I had become personally involved with these gentle people. I confess freely that my judgment was impaired secondary to my emotional state and I lacked the counterbalancing wisdom of Tula, who normally would have served as my conscience.

Leader was preparing the group to move in a southern direction. Without the understanding that the changes to the sky were global in nature, they believed they could simply walk away from the encroachment of the dark and cold. I believed this to be a futile move but had no other feasible options to bring to the table. In any case, my influence on the decision would have been negligible.

Outside of the relative security of the cave, the temperature had dropped dramatically and this effect was felt even more keenly each day that passed. Days were spent working to exhaustion, the tribe overcoming their fear in order to make two more kills of elk, wrapping the meat in hides and gathering their meager belongings for the anticipated relocation. I hovered near Flower, having learned to love her as a surrogate mother, my own having been deceased for many years. She would, in her intuitive and gentle manner, know just when to reach her hand out and touch mine with her rough and calloused one. With a nod of her head, as if to remind me to get back to work, she would nudge me along. My sorrow was intensified in that I privately decided to not accompany the tribe on their journey. I believed their struggle against nature to be hopeless, but that was not my rationale for staying behind. Without my *symbiont,* Tula, I could not return to my century. If I made my way south with the tribe, I would have been a burden on them, requiring valuable resources for survival. Also, as they aged, I would not; there was no desire in me to watch my friends grow old and die, leaving me behind again and again. If I had to face the future alone, it was my preference to stay put, since there was no logical reason to choose another course of action. Perhaps part of my thinking was entirely selfish in nature, but then no one ever said that *symbionts* could not be self serving.

The day finally came when preparations were finalized and Leader decided, along with the elders, that it was time to leave. As the group started to gather their carefully prepared packs which were mounted on several travois, I hung back. Flower quickly looked at me, her intuitive skills revealing my intent. Tears, a rarity, sprung to her dark eyes. She began, with the guttural language of which I had acquired a rudimentary knowledge, trying to convince me to come with the group. Overhearing her urgent phrases, the story of my staying behind quickly moved through the camp and the people became agitated. Finally, Leader came to me and tried to take my hand to gently pull me towards the slowly moving group. I smiled, patted his hand and pulled away.

Flower told the others she would not leave me behind and emphasized the point by promptly sitting down on the dusty earth, dropping her pack to the ground with finality. Leader looked at us, consternation on his weathered face, not certain what to do with two oppositional females. I solved his problem by picking up the pack, pulling Flower to her feet and firmly indicating with gestures that she should rejoin the group. Reminding her that Leader was in charge, I indicated that she must follow his guidance. Several others gathered about her in a circle and finally persuaded her to move with the rest of them. The last I saw of my adoptive family was their little group disappearing over a hill, moving steadily southward.

They left me some food, even though I had insisted they not dip into their crucial stores for me. With metabolic needs different than a human's, *symbionts* can survive much longer without nourishment. Returning to the cave, I carefully stoked the fire, not wanting to lose its precious warmth. As I lay back on my elk hide, an idea returned to me, one I had envisioned a few nights previously. This group of humans was quite prolific in cave painting, and I knew from my historical research prior to this time shift, that these caves were discovered in the late 1800's with much public interest. The pictures were later widely distributed all about the world. I decided to add to the text of the paintings, leaving my own message there, too, in the unique language of *symbionts*. Maybe one day, someone from my group would see the painting, recognize the notation and be able to record my outcome in the historical record. It was not unheard of, and fellow travelers had been known to leave a similar imprint in the past. It was our way of marking events and was a type of humorous "Kilroy was here" moment in time. Thus, I wrote on the cave walls, using plant matter that had been crushed and diluted as paint pigment, to make my mark in history next to the crude but beautiful pictures of bison, elk and other animals of the tundra.

Having done this, there was nothing left for me to do but wait, reflect and be observant. I actually placed myself in a meditative state, not quite hibernation, but something fairly close. A hallmark of my kind is a slow metabolism and a naturally long life. Prolonged passage of time did not evoke anxiety as it might have in a human.

I found, in my suspended state, that I dreamt almost constantly. In my mind, I relived many of my past journeys, recalled acquaintances and relationships, and, most of all, I thought of my dear Tula. Not being a scientist, I was uncertain how we had evolved as we did. But all I did know was that we symbiotic beings had evolved, our life lines paralleling that of humans. And, despite my physical appearance of being human, I am not, and my genetic counterpart is my lupine *symbiont*. Despite a difference in physical appearance, Tula and I were almost genetically identical. Telepaths, we had the ability to establish a symbiotic link which enabled us to travel through time. Tula possessed all of my intelligence, her development focusing on intuitive energy, instinct and emotion. She would have enjoyed my long life with me, growing old together, had not her life been cut short by placing herself in danger to protect me. At the time of her death, I was somewhere in the midst of young adulthood and had the potential to be matched with a new *symbiont*, that is, if I were home.

As the days passed, I realized I had never been alone like this. Being one of a species of *symbionts*, I had always been in telepathic connection with another like being. Even after Tula died, I was able to feel a connection with the human tribe who had adopted me. Searching their minds, I could discern feelings, impressions, and sensations. I found myself, totally alone, for the first time in my life. It was mildly disturbing, like being a piece in a big puzzle with multiple pieces missing. Not a complete whole was I.

Wrapping myself in one of the elk hides, I focused and reached out with my mind. All that was to be done now was to be patient and wait for an uncertain destiny.

CHAPTER 2

The days passed in a seamless succession. The waning summer, with its former warmth and abundance of life, evolved quickly into what resembled late fall edging towards early winter. Keeping close to the cave, I used the meager stores of food that had been left by my insistent friends. Also, I did some careful foraging and was fortunate to find some nuts and roots that helped to sustain me. On occasion, I marked the passage of animals—some large herbivores such as bison and elk—which seemed to be following a migratory path southwards. More rarely, I saw predators, bears and cave lions, who were trailing after the rapidly disappearing food sources. One afternoon, as I lay curled under a soft hide trying to warm myself beside the small fire I constantly fed, there was a loud snuffling sound at the entrance of the cave. Reaching out with my mind, I recognized the primitive cognitions of a bear. My telepathic talents were only truly useful with another telepath, one who could project thoughts and feelings for me to receive. But I did have the ability to take the measure of a *nonsymbiont*—in this case, a mother bear, burdened by a trio of cubs, a rarity. Her stress was palpable, as the precipitous changes in weather were signaling it was time to hibernate. Her fat stores were insufficient for the extended winter which loomed, and her cubs' demands were too great. Cautiously coming into view, she sensed me and turned her massive head to better regard me with one unblinking brown eye. In the semidarkness, her face was flat, one dimensional, and without expression. Then, with a grunt, she retreated, just as cautiously, taking her cubs away from what she perceived to be an unsafe situation.

Clambering to my feet, I went to the entrance of the cave and watched as she lumbered off, trailed by her happy, gamboling trio. After moving about 100 yards to the southwest, she made her way up a small incline where there was another series of caves, where she and her family could establish residence. My compassion for this struggling mother overwhelmed me, and it was at this point I obviously gave up any serious attempt at long term survival. I was not conscious of this, but my actions spoke volumes. Returning to my place by the fire, I used a small scrap of hide to gather up most of the collected nuts and roots and, picking my way carefully down the hillside, I took them to within ten yards of the mouth of the bears' new den. Scurrying quickly off, I turned to watch from a safe distance. Within a short time, the mother bear appeared at the cave's entrance and walked out, her head swinging side to side, nose in the air. In a moment, she located the little treasure store and, joined by her cubs, they all buried their muzzles in the pile of food. I felt a stab of joy at having made a small difference in a hostile and unaccommodating world.

After the initial feeding of the bears, I spent my days looking for nuts, roots, dried berries, anything at all, before it disappeared in the changing climate. In an odd way, this gave me purpose and dispelled my sense of solitude and despair. My carefully collected booty would then be taken to the same location and left for my ursine friends. They were, of course, wild, and would warily watch me from a distance as they foraged. And I was cautious, knowing that one of the most dangerous and unpredictable creature on earth is a mother bear with cubs. But the minute I would withdraw to my hillock, they would descend upon the piled up food. I was simply grateful to have any distraction.

But in time, as the weather cooled even more, the mother bear made the decision to take her cubs into the cave for the remainder of the season, and they abandoned me at that point. It is difficult to explain the degree of solitude I felt when I could no longer glance up and see the cubs falling all over one another and engaging in mock battles. There was also sadness on my part, for I knew what the bear did not: she would emerge from a premature hibernation, not having had time to adequately prepare her body. Leaving her cave, there would be no food; the water would be contaminated from silt. The bear and her cubs would die of starvation.

On one particularly blustery day, I sat on a hill that had become my favorite place, where I faced west and watched the glimmer of what would have been a setting sun behind the curtain of dust that still obscured the sky. Sitting there, deep in contemplation, my arms wrapped around my knees which were hugged tightly to my chest, I felt a tingling, as if someone or something was knocking at the doorway of my mind. It had been so long since I had felt a telepathic contact that I had to concentrate and try and make certain this was not a hallucination. No, there it was again, a subtle but very evident sensation. Somebody out there was searching for me. I struggled to my feet, now physically weak from insufficient food and the constant ache of being cold, that no elk hide or carefully tended fire could bank. All I could do was focus my thoughts outward and beckon my unknown friend to come to me. Standing in the cool wind until darkness had overtaken the land, at last I retreated to the cave, tending to my fire and continuing to project my thoughts. On and off for hours, I would feel the gentle touch of a probing mind, connect, and just as quickly withdraw; my unknown suitor was cautious.

Exhaustion finally claimed me and caused me to sink
down in weary repose on my elk hide. Deep sleep
enveloped me, despite my attempts to stay awake and
focused. Several hours must have passed when I startled
awake, sitting up abruptly, pushing the hide off my legs,
eyes wide open, searching the semi darkness of my cave.
There was a developing awareness of a keen mind,
intensely curious thoughts, and then a presence hovering
in the darkness off to my left. I was not alone.

"Who are you?" I asked with my mind, my species
having found spoken language to be an inadequate,
imprecise and unnecessary form of communication.

A pair of amber eyes, ringed with dark fur, slanted and
exotic, peered back at me, glowing in the subtle light of
the small fire. I was completely transfixed as the beast's
mind reached out to touch mine with reassurance. But
even with that, I could tell he was as startled to find me
as I was him.

"I heard you call out and I came for you," he answered,
stepping forward so that the flickering light from my fire
sparked a display of color reflected off his dense, reddish
hued coat.

In response, I am ashamed to say that I just collapsed,
my shoulders shaking as I began to cry uncontrollably.
My solitude had been so absolute, that this sudden and
unexpected meeting with a fellow *symbiont* left me
emotionally shaken. Distressed at my emotional display,
my new friend moved rapidly to my side, his auburn fur
rippling over his sleek body. He appeared to be well
nourished and healthy, so he had somehow figured out
how to flourish despite the compromised times in which
we lived. Falling back on my elk hide, I tried to compose
myself. My new companion drew close and placed his
long muzzle on my outstretched arm and crouched low,
doing his best to comfort me, this genetic brother of
mine.

We stayed that way for a time, sorting each other out
with gentle explorations of our minds. I quickly realized

that my new friend, though kind in nature, was inexperienced with that sort of sharing. He told me of the loss of his mother, she having been the only one of our kind with whom he had a relationship, and his subsequent solitary existence for the past 200 plus winters. I was ashamed of my self pity over my relatively short time in isolation. This *symbiont* was made of sturdier material than was I.

"My mother called me Kipp," he shared. "And you are?" he paused, waiting for my reply.

"I am Petra," I replied.

He made a soft sound in response and curled a little closer to me. I realized that Kipp had not experienced any physical contact for a very long time and draped my hand along the back of his neck and gently caressed his thick pelt of fur. Sighing, he closed those amazing amber eyes and attempted to nestle even closer as he rested his muzzle across my chest.

After a while, Kipp asked me, "Why Petra?" He turned his head slightly to look at my face. His thoughts flickered and it was clear he was still reconciling the fact that a fellow *symbiont* could look human. Kipp's mother might have told him stories of such things but seeing the reality of it was another matter.

"Of all my mother's journeys, she preferred the ancient city of Petra, thinking it was the most fascinating edifice ever built," I answered. "So when I was born, she wanted to name me after something she had loved and cherished." Pausing, I raised myself on my elbow to better examine my new companion.

Kipp, in turn, permitted himself to gaze at me in curiosity. His mother had told him of us—of her humanoid companion who had been killed. Kipp's mind was filled with confusion; the physical similarities between me, a humanoid *symbiont,* and the human species –who had been less than accepting of him—were clearly at odds with his limited experiences.

"I know that they've hunted you, fearful that you're a

predator," I said aloud, in response to his thoughts. My voice was slightly croaky due to disuse. He gave a soft murmur. Continuing with my thoughts, I said, "This is a dangerous time; people are primitive and reactive." Pausing, I added, "You know, we may look alike, humans and myself, but I'm not human. You and I, however, are alike, despite our physical appearances."

Kipp apparently made a decision about me—about us—for he suddenly rose, and, after a lengthy stretch both fore and aft, he asked, "How long has it been since you have eaten?" Without waiting for an answer, he loped quickly from the cave into the pale light of early sunrise. It was not too long before he returned, carrying in his jaws two large mountain trout. His coat was damp from his efforts and I motioned him close to the fire. Using a cutting stone left behind by my humanoid friends, I was able to clean the trout and prepare a small breakfast for us on the spit. Kipp was clearly uncertain about eating the cooked fish, his experience having been with raw flesh, so he ate with caution, his lips drawn back from his teeth, resulting in a comical expression. I finally had to laugh out loud. Kipp looked at me, startled, having never heard such a sound. Reading my feeling tone, he realized the playfulness, and, lolling his tongue out, he gave a good impression of a canine laugh in response.

Symbionts that time shift are carefully matched and then have an extended period of time in which to learn each other's characteristics, temperament, and the cadence and patterns of thoughts. Consequently, it was uncertain if Kipp and I could achieve the connection that was normally the end product of a crafted process. But here we were, and since there was nothing else to do, it seemed reasonable to work towards a mutual goal. I wanted to return home and Kipp had no reason to remain in this hostile, solitary land, where he had no family or companions. He was excited to learn more of his heritage and I had only hinted at his potential, not wanting to skew the outcome. Over the next few weeks, I began a gradual education, in between our constant searches for the quickly evaporating food sources.

"So, where did we come from?" he asked one evening, as we settled down by the ever burning fire, he taking his now familiar position at my side, muzzle across my chest.

"Well, all I know is what I was taught," I replied. "My mother believed there is a supreme maker –many refer to this being as God—and He put the divine spark of life in all creatures with whom we share this world. So, He created us, too. For reasons best explained by those who understand biology and science, we *symbionts* spawned in a different pool and are of the same makeup as one another, despite our physical differences."

Kipp looked at my hands and then glanced down at his paws.

"Is one of us superior to the other?" he asked. Kipp's total lack of artifice, his honesty and genuine nature were enduring qualities that drew my admiration.

I smiled and replied, "No, but our appearances have enabled us to interact in different ways within cultures, as you'll see one day when we're able to go to the future. To humans, I look like another human being, and to them you look like a canine animal."

Kipp's thoughts raced ahead and I was struck –and not for the first or last time—by his intelligence and ability to process information. He put many I had known to shame with his superior mind.

"My mother, when she was dying, told me to 'Be good'. Are we, good?" he asked, stumbling a little in his query.

I paused a moment before saying, "Kipp, I don't think you need to have any concerns about your goodness. Now I'm another matter," I said, with a soft laugh. "But in general our species has evolved to avoid using our skills in ways that are harmful. *Symbionts,* through our telepathic gifts and ability to time shift—or travel through time—have a naturally unfair advantage over humans. Not all of us have been good historically, but we have hopefully learned important lessons and try to ensure we do no harm. We have rules we impose upon ourselves that are supposed to regulate our actions, to make certain we do the right thing." I paused and ran my hands over his ears, which were pricked up in an attentive posture.

"Do you understand that since we possess the ability to travel in time, a *symbiont* could go back in history and actually intervene to change the progress of the world?"

"Why would anyone want to do that?" he asked.

I realized that living as he had, in such a primitive time, he had developed no concept of wealth, power, avarice, or acquisition. From his point of view, there would be no reason to change events. Searching my mind, I looked for an analogy he would comprehend.

"Kipp, you have watched the wolf packs and see that there's one alpha in control of the others. That same idea applies here. Humans tend to control resources and each other. *Symbionts* are not perfect creatures and can fall prey to greed and the need for power."

His eyes widened as understanding of his potential flooded his mind. I listened carefully to the flow and heard only his astonishment that any being could stoop to that level of corruptness. Never once did he pause to consider how he might use his abilities to enrich himself. That was promising, and I felt encouraged that Kipp had the necessary elements to mesh within the *symbiont* society that was the end result of thousands of years of history and experiences.

CHAPTER 3

As time passed, Kipp and I continued to work together, both on fundamental survival as well as our growth as a symbiotic pair. Kipp proved to be a resourceful hunter, having certain natural abilities that I did not share, due to his exceptional senses of sight, hearing and smell. My job was to continue to look for what few roots could be found, while Kipp hunted for protein, usually fish, which could still be located in nearby waters but in rapidly declining numbers. We had not seen any herbivorous animals for a few weeks and realized that we needed to perfect our symbiosis so that we could move forward in time before we faced starvation. Kipp shared my slow metabolism, a characteristic of our species, and he could survive for even longer periods than could I without food, as long as there was abundant water. Fortunately for us, there was a small spring fed pool of water in the cave that had been spared from the contaminating silt that was ever present.

One day as we were away from the relative safety of our cave, I traveled down a small gulley looking for anything edible. The weather was now cold, and I had wrapped one of the worn hides about my shoulders in a feeble effort to stay warm. The once nurturing tundra had evolved into a harsh and unforgiving environment.

A brisk wind cut through the elk hide and I turned my face from the spray of fine sand that whipped against my flesh. Spying something peeking from the hardened soil, I bent forward eagerly with my digging tool to try and pry the object loose from the earth's tenacious grasp. It looked to be a root plant, edible, possibly, and I dug with fervor. From behind me, there was a faint clatter of stones and I whirled about to find a pair of wolves who had stumbled upon me. The thought occurred that they were looking for food, too.

My mind must have sent off an alarm, although I rapidly tried to suppress it, fearful that Kipp would respond and put himself in danger—the nightmare of Tula's death had never left me. As the wolves began a purposeful and steady approach towards me, I looked in desperation for anything that could be used for self defense.

Bending to pick up a rock, I stumbled backwards as the alpha wolf lunged towards me. At that moment, a reddish blur appeared from my left side, knocking me to the ground. It was Kipp, who took position in front of me, his massive head low to the ground, fangs exposed, hackles raised. His thoughts were focused and there was no uncertainty or fear in him at all. The wolves, as a block, moved back a step or two, confounded by this new dynamic in the equation. The instinctive abilities of the wolves told them that this was no mere wolf or dog and they were fearful of Kipp; I could read this much in their primitive minds. Kipp read it, too, and took the opportunity to advance on the alpha male, snapping his jaws in the air and thrusting his head forward.

Sprawled on the ground watching this showdown unwind, a change began to come over me. My eyes clouded, a tint coming down like a veil over my vision, coating the scene in tones of umber. My breathing changed, and, looking down, I saw that the hair on my arms was standing on end; likewise, I could feel the hair rising on my scalp and neck. It was at that moment that my entire view of the situation changed, and I was seeing the scenario through Kipp's eyes. My sight became focused tunnel vision as the alpha wolf became the target of my view. A pounding, racing pulse was audible in my ears. Taking a breath, I could smell the wolves—their uncertainty, as well as their fear of Kipp. In the highly charged energy of the moment, Kipp and I had become one, a symbiotic fusion of our previous selves. Kipp's ears twitched backward towards me and it was evident he felt it, too. What normally took *symbionts* months or even years to achieve through practice and focused meditation and guidance had occurred between us in this moment, in the context of high emotion.

Thankfully, the wolves decided that, despite the hunger that gnawed at their bellies, we were too much work as a food source, and they turned to canter back down the scrub filled wash, their paws churning up little dust puffs as they disappeared from view. Kipp watched after them, vigilant, until his senses told him that they were truly gone. I felt his entire being relax, my body doing so in kind. Kipp turned to look at me, amazement written all over his expressive face.

"So this is what it's like," he commented sitting back on his haunches. He was clearly fascinated with his innocent intrusion into my mind, and I understood he lacked the customary boundaries and reserve that modern day *symbionts* had acquired in order to coexist in a civilized society.

"Yes," I paused for a moment, still rather shaken by the event and struggling to separate myself from Kipp's psyche. It had been so long since I had joined with another *symbiont,* that recovering my discipline was done with effort. Kipp would, with time, learn the balance of symbiosis... the art of engagement while maintaining one's individuality. The actual merging was an act above and beyond telepathy, something we found to be as natural as breathing.

Kipp walked to my side, his eyes half closed against the ever present wind. He rested his soft muzzle on my shoulder, the closest approximation he had to an embrace. As I followed his thoughts, they shifted unexpectedly to his mother and I noted the gentle flow, feeling his love for her and the pangs of longing for her. Placing my arm about his neck, I pulled him even closer, pressing my face against his ruddy pelt.

"She would be proud of her little boy," I told him. Yes, indeed.

Later, in subsequent days as Kipp and I practiced symbiotic melding and separation, I gradually introduced him to additional history of our species and exactly where we fit in the universe.

"We have worked diligently to coexist in a human dominated world, to seamlessly look and act human, lest they discover who is living in their midst. We may look like them, or at least some of us do, but our long lives would cause suspicion. So we move about in society, staying only long enough to work among groups of humans and leave before they recognize we are not aging with them."

"And what about the canines?" Kipp asked, as we lay in the cave, close to our crackling fire, while the winds howled outside in the dark.

"Well, in the future, the world is dominated by humans, over a billion of them. From their viewpoint, all other animals are lesser beings, not sentient, and some they consider to be companions, or what they refer to as pets. Canines fit into that group of pets." I paused, glancing at him.

Tilting his head, Kipp asked, "So what does it mean to be a pet to a human?"

That was a difficult one. The ever curious Kipp was keeping me on my toes, now and probably for the next several hundred years.

"Kipp, people are as different in their beliefs as are we. Some value animals as companions and love them with ferocity. They buy collars and leashes and take them to parks for walks."

"What's a collar and leash?" he asked, clearly confounded by all of this.

"A collar fits around a dog's neck and then the leash is a cord that attaches the dog to the human so he won't get lost or wander off."

Kipp's eyes were wide open. "So you mean that humans would want to put something around my neck and force me to stay with them?" At my affirmative nod, he asked, "Would it hurt me?"

"Kipp, since you have the appearance of a dog, you will blend in with more ease in human society. With your telepathic gifts and intelligence, you will be safe, since they will perpetually underestimate you. I have always envied the canine branch of our family tree for those reasons."

Kipp's agile mind was in play, busy hatching his next question.

"Why do you think we bonded as we have? From what you've told me, it is usually a much more complicated and time consuming event."

"I'm not a scientist or geneticist, but I think that we more closely approximate what was natural for our species some 100,000 years ago. My understanding is that due to the relatively small number of *symbionts* on earth, something called genetic degradation has occurred. In other words, in any species, if there are insufficient numbers to keep the gene pool diverse, there'll be breakdowns in the gene structure and then anomalies occur over time. An impolite term might be inbreeding." I paused, giving him time to consider what I had said, before continuing. "And many of our contemporary scientists believe this to be the root cause for the fact that our ability to bond and time travel is becoming a rarity. You would, of course, have a pure gene structure and thus have greater abilities than would I or any of my contemporaries."

Kipp's mental brow was creased in vertical furrows. "You have told me that it is important for us to blend in with the human species. I still don't understand why we have to conceal our presence from them."

This did not lend itself to a simple explanation. And I did not want to confuse the issues as it would be a disadvantage to him if he was fearful of humans.

"Kipp, there are some extremely fine people in the world, so I don't want you to think that humans are our enemies. But people, as a block, are often fearful of things they cannot understand. In ancient times, as well as during the Middle Ages, we were in danger of extermination because people thought we had supernatural powers, which would have been considered to be demonic gifts." I paused for a moment to dig out a pebble which had been biting into my lower back.

"Demonic stuff in the Middle Ages was not good at all. The accused would end up on a pile of rushes while someone threw a lit match to the vigorous applause of onlookers. Anyway, now we are more at risk of being used by unscrupulous people to alter historic events so that those people can gain riches, power, control, etc."

I knew this would not be enough information for him.

"Let me give you a more specific example. There was a serious conflict in the twentieth century, a war called World War Two. It was a classic conflict between good and evil. A *symbiont*, with the knowledge of the end result—which is that good prevailed—could go back and, let's say, change the equation at several critical points and completely alter the outcome of the war. The world and humanity would have evolved differently and the fascists would have ruled the world."

There was sorrow in Kipp's expressive eyes as he looked at me.

"Petra, are there any of us who would do something like that?" It was apparent that his mother had imprinted her own set of ethics on her child, and it bode well for him to have such values in troubled times. I was not an ethicist but had strong feelings on the matter.

"Kipp, this is one of the most important things I can ever tell you: each and every one of us has the potential to be corrupted. It is only through our knowledge of this potential that we remain humble and hopefully don't fall into the pit."

He struggled, not wanting to ask me, but finally he did.

"Have you ever been tempted to do things you shouldn't?"

"Yes, I have, and when that happened, I shared it with Tula and some others who are close to me and whom I can trust. I considered their counsel and hopefully did the right thing."

Kipp tilted his head back as he looked at me.

"So, will I be the one you ask, now that Tula is gone?"

"Kipp, I can't think of anyone I would trust more to be my superego. I doubt you'll struggle with your demons as much as do I." He started to object, but I cut him off. "No, it's okay to be humble. But let's face it: you are just naturally possessed of a good nature. You, however, will have to become accustomed to the community of *symbionts* wanting to oversee your activities. It, unfortunately, is a necessary evil, since we don't all possess the ability to self regulate as we should."

Kipp, who had spent his existence to date in a free and unfettered manner, expressed some dismay at the idea of an all controlling body that would tell him what to do. Reaching out, I pulled him close and hugged him to my chest.

"It's not that bad, Kipp. You have been on your own so long that it may seem odd, but even packs of wolves have rules of order so that they can survive."

He grudgingly acknowledged the truth in my words.

We realized that we needed to achieve the ability to time shift and this must happen soon. The first step had been made, in that we had formed a symbiotic fusion. The climate was worsening daily and food sources were almost exhausted. Outside of our cave, the world looked wasted. The trees, minus any vegetation, were skeletal in appearance. The sun, such a powerful source of life, was totally defeated by the dust cloud that surrounded the earth.

In an attempt to stretch our meager resources, we resorted to eating only every fourth day. My metabolism was not slow enough for this sort of deprivation, and I was losing weight, albeit slowly. Something would have to change and quickly. Kipp, bless him, never uttered any complaint. Each day he went out, braving the cold, dim world, to search for anything remotely edible. I, too, would go, wrapped in my elk hide, but confess the cold was getting the better of me. Lacking Kipp's naturally insulating warm pelt, my body ached as the relentless wind beat down on me like needles made of ice. This day was particularly savage, and I staggered back to the cave, weak, and feeling the freeze to my core. In a short time Kipp arrived, and, after staring at me with concern, he crawled over my prone form and used his warmth to stave off my shivers. Eventually, enough of the chill receded so that I fell into a light sleep. Some hours later I jerked awake. Kipp had removed his heavy bulk and lay next to me in his customary pose, muzzle stretched across my chest. Opening an amber eye, he subjected me to a cursory examination.

"Petra," he began, "I was afraid last night. You looked so weak...." His thoughts drifted off. Although he tried to control the wanderings of his mind, they darted to the memory of his mother as she slipped away from him.

Trying to sound unconcerned, I brushed away his worry.

"I'm fine, Kipp."

His eyes opened wide as he responded. "No, you aren't fine. You are depleted. I can sense that much. We need to be done with this place and make our way to your home and soon." Standing, he stretched his body, engaged in a long, aggressive shake and then sat on his haunches. Clearly he was ready to get to work. "So, what do we do?"

I was almost too tired and weak, but knew I had to try. There was no way on heaven or earth that I would let Kipp down after all he had done for me.

"I only know that in the past, I would concentrate fully on my home—its appearance, the familiar surroundings—and that would become a beacon for me to direct my movement." I answered his question before he could formulate it. "And the ability to find home is not unheard of in other species. Dogs have found their way after journeys of hundreds of miles. Whales return to breeding grounds after thousand miles journeys. Even little hummingbirds migrate for long distances. No one knows how they do it, but they do, as do we."

"But Tula was familiar with your destination—home—and I am not."

That did pose a challenge for us.

"I will flood my mind with every conceivable memory I have of home in all the minute detail I can conjure. You will have to learn home from my memories. I don't think this is the usual way this is done, but your enhanced abilities should help compensate for the liabilities we have."

We spent the remainder of the day and the next two in that fashion, meditative, with me feeding him memories of home. In my mind, I would walk us up to the front door of my small house, turn the heavy brass door knob and in we would go, walking from one room to another. I would pause, gazing at the worn honey toned oak plank flooring, noting the bright colors of scattered rugs which broke up the monotone surface. Together we wandered from room to room, looking at the eclectic combinations of antique furniture, mixed in with discards, hand me downs, and other bits and pieces. None of it matched or should have fit together, but somehow it managed.

I enjoyed Kipp's amazement at my memories of the future, which painted a picture of profound contrast to his primitive experiences. We continually practiced meditation and deep, synchronized breathing. Kipp's natural talents made the process flow in a manner I had never experienced with Tula. The time finally came when he and I both felt we were as ready as possible to attempt the time shift.

"Kipp, relax yourself and begin breathing deeply and slowly." In response to my command, he began doing as I bade him. "Okay, that is excellent. Now, start working on connecting with me and fill your mind with the thoughts I have of home and concentrate on flowing movement."

I followed suit and after a while found myself in a state of deep relaxation. My sense of being and Kipp's were beginning to merge. The interior of the now familiar cave began to darken, the edges blurring, and the gentle sounds of the crackling fire, which was in dire contrast to the roaring of the wind outside, began to blend into a soft rushing noise that increased in intensity. The actual movement felt like one was falling into a funnel—the world, once large and expansive, was gradually narrowing to a fine point. I could feel Kipp, both physically, my hands twisted into his fur, and mentally, his mind engaged with mine. It was thus we made our first journey together.

CHAPTER 4

My memories and reflections pushed me into a deep sleep. Reluctantly, I awoke to the ambient light that was beginning to illuminate the bedroom with the coming of dawn. My arm was thrown over Kipp's back, and I could feel his heavy warmth, the easy rise and fall of his even breaths. He turned his massive head and gazed at me with one open eye. I could feel his tail thumping the mattress with happiness and contentment. Awakening here was preferable to the cold dirt packed floor of the cave we had left.

The chance meeting between me and Kipp in the remote past had stretched the odds of such a thing as happening to the level of miraculous. I had pondered the issue of such— are there truly miracles or is there just good and bad luck? But such debates were better left to theologians, or at least to deeper thinkers than was I. It was enough for me to simply be grateful for the wonderful Kipp, who literally saved my life.

"Well, Kipp," I began, "we need to eat and then start making ready to go to meet the others."

He asked me to prepare him more fully for what was ahead, and, since I was still feeling lazy and in no particular hurry to leave the comfort of my bed, I began an abbreviated history of the evolution of the company we called Technicorps.

"There is a decision making body of twelve humanoids and canines, and they vote on issues and serve as the conscience of the group. We have subsidiaries all over the planet, with pods of *symbionts* that coexist and work with human beings worldwide. The humans, of course, don't know our true origins, so we move around frequently from company to company so that our different aging processes will go undetected." I paused for a moment and continued, "We have companies that work on renewable energy sources, research into disease states and treatment and cures for a number of illnesses; we also provide colleges and universities with lecturers who can help educate and advance knowledge to the human species."

Kipp was having difficulty following my train of thought since the technology of the present day world was beyond his experience, so I slowed down and flooded my mind with more complete pictures to help him comprehend.

"Petra, what I don't understand is why the *symbionts* of your time seem to, well, dote on humans and want to serve them. When I was a pup, all I recall is that we were fearful of humans and tried to stay away from them as much as possible. They were savage and primitive."

I pulled him close to me again, and he rubbed his head against my shoulder.

"All of this is difficult to explain, but you will recall that humans have evolved as a species over the past 75,000 years or so. So we must be patient with them and not expect them to be who we are. Kipp, we *symbionts,* as a consequence of our evolution, have become a disciplined, emotionally controlled species; later I will tell you more, but believe me when I tell you that we have been involved in past episodes of tampering with history with disastrous results. We cannot ever allow ourselves to alter the path of history in any way."

Kipp asked, "But what is it about them you seem to like so much?"

"They possess all the spontaneity and recklessness that

we lack, and they have a singularly unique relationship with God. According to my mother, God created the world and all the creatures on earth including us, but God chose man to be in his image." I paused in my thoughts to let Kipp mull this over. "At one time, *symbionts* became envious of man due to his special relationship with God. We were in great danger of allowing our envy to corrupt us as we attempted to gain a greater position in God's eyes; we wanted to be greater than humanity." Puzzled over my shame, an emotion he had not yet experienced in his young life, he gave me a quick glance before resting his head back across my chest.

"But we, after having made many missteps, found our place in the universe. We try to conduct ourselves in such a way to better the world in which we live." I thought about it a moment and added, "We *symbionts* had to learn humility, which was difficult, given our advanced capabilities."

We finally got up, and while Kipp padded to the kitchen to exit the house through the dog door to take care of his needs, I made a bathroom visit to do the same. It was interesting to find how much more pleasurable it was to be able to use a commode on demand versus my experience of the preceding two years of locating a bush in the tundra for such. Modern day technology was definitely preferable in my vast experience, and since I had been assigned to many primitive locales during my career, I thought I knew what I was talking about.

After a few minutes, Kipp and I met back up in the kitchen. While I tried to find something we could eat— and the cupboards were shockingly bare, as was the refrigerator—Kipp wandered around the house to better acquaint himself with objects that were unfamiliar to a cave dwelling *symbiont*. As I pulled together some foods, his mind would reach out to me as he located another treasure or mystery and convey the thought in pictures for me to give an explanation. For a moment, I had the happy feeling that it was much like being the mother to a toddler—my relationship to Kipp—with the endless questions, and asking 'why' over and over again. But I was of a patient nature, and this sort of energy flow was acceptable to me.

I had a small television, dusty from lack of use, and that particular object drew Kipp's curiosity. Since he lacked opposable thumbs, I left the kitchen and went to the living room to turn it on, thinking it would be interesting to see what happened. Kipp was startled when a face materialized and out of the talking head came the local news of the day. As was true of all lupine *symbionts*, he could not comprehend the spoken language since there were no thoughts attached for him to register. Even when I spoke out loud to him, he was only reading my thoughts and not my spoken words.

I returned to the kitchen to continue to work on a meal; as I did so, I tried to share my limited knowledge of electricity, light bulbs, television, plumbing—in particular, Kipp was drawn to the whirlpool like action of a flushed toilet—and found, as I did so, that I had taken way too many things for granted. The food, pitiful as it was, was ready and we had a small meal.

Afterwards, Kipp followed me to the bathroom and watched in fascination as I turned on water to the shower. He curled up on the rug while I bathed with great pleasure, this being my first real bath with soap and warm water in a long time. Upon my exit from the tub, he stared at my naked body with curiosity; I could read his thoughts, his humor at how, well, hair distribution was different on the body of a humanoid versus that of a canine.

"I understand now why you have to wear those coverings over your bodies."

I quickly dressed and politely inquired if Kipp wanted me to groom him, not wanting to be insulting, but he did look pretty rough. His eyes widened a bit, following my thoughts of having bathed Tula in the bathtub, something she had enjoyed. His response was immediately negative, so I proceeded on to inquiring if he would like to be brushed or combed. Having no frame of reference, he was hesitant, so I compared this simple act with his mother having bathed him when he was young.

Startled, he asked, "You mean you are going to clean me with your tongue?"

I had to laugh at that and held up the brush. He paused but finally allowed me to proceed and quickly found that he enjoyed the gentle touch of the bristles. Soon I had a small mountain of discarded hair, burrs and brambles and he gleamed like a copper penny. There was one full length mirror and I let Kipp inspect himself for the first time. He was amazed to see his tall, lean body, the amber eyes ringed with dark fur staring back at his reflection.

I left him there—parading back and forth, staring over his shoulder as he retreated, trying to catch his reflection as he turned around—and went to my small study to look at the piled up mail carefully collected by Philo in my absence. Almost all the junk stuff had been tossed already, leaving a few bills. My visit to the past had lasted about 30 months, but in terms of how much actual time had elapsed at home, I had only been gone a month. All of that depended on the imprecise nature of the time shift. Some pros could shift, go back in time and remain years, and return to their contemporary setting on the same day. I admit I lacked that talent and was simply not that good.

It only took me a few moments to sort through and determine which pieces of correspondence needed immediate attention. I wrote out a few bills, thinking that I could post them on my way to work. Kipp was suspiciously silent; I canvassed the air for his thoughts and found him, quiet, but curious, so he seemed okay for the moment. After I finished, I returned to my bedroom.

Kipp was lying quietly on the rug, still staring at that mirror.

"Kipp, are you obsessed, or what?" I laughed, feeling the need to jest with him a little.

"I feel like I have found a brother," he replied with humor.

I joined him, sitting down, with my legs crossed, on the small rug. He looked at our shared reflection, and I knew he was still processing all that had transpired during our relatively short association.

"There is no good explanation for the differences in our appearances." I gestured to my mirrored image as I spoke. "Nature is wise, and I believe there is always a purpose, but she doesn't have to share her reasons with the little folk."

"I think I would rather have four legs," he said, "because I can run so much faster than you. And I like the fur, because I don't have to spend all the time putting on an artificial layer of protection before I go out." He turned his head to glance at my hands. "But I do wish I had hands like yours, because you can do much more with them than I can with my paws."

I ruffled his head fur and stood. Crossing the room to a desk, I rambled through a drawer, until I found a worn leather slip lead, explaining to Kipp that we would have to adopt the role in public of his being a dog. He was not particularly happy about having a piece of leather encircling his neck but understood the need for the charade. We would shortly be at the institute, and I had done all I could do to prepare Kipp for this new journey.

CHAPTER 5

Philo Marshall sat back in his chair, stretching his cramped back, tired after several hours of sitting at the large table surrounded by his *symbiont* peers. This group worked as a collective, voting democratically on issues that came before them. But Philo, due to his age and experience, was the de facto leader, and the group typically honored his lead. His current level of fatigue was making it more difficult to focus and keep his usual guard over his thoughts. Being a telepath had its ups and downs.

Across the table sat Max Stone, a younger male, capable but ambitious, who fancied himself the successor to Philo. The fact that he did not command the same respect had always caused him to have some degree of bitterness. With his saturnine good looks and natural charisma, however, he was the obvious candidate to eventually ease into the leadership position at whatever point in time Philo was no longer able or willing to serve. Max was a skilled enough politician to keep his darker plans of power and acquisition closeted in the deep recesses of his mind lest any of the other telepaths access his thoughts. Maybe humans as a species appreciated aggression and power, but *symbionts* had long ago taken another path. However, even among them, there would be those who took an aberrant journey.

"So, when can we expect Petra to grace us with her presence?" Max began, smiling to offset his agitation.

Philo glanced at Max, his dark eyes somber beneath heavy, grizzled brows. He had long been fond of Petra, serving as her mentor and champion. Max knew this and was needling him unnecessarily.

"She was asking for some time to rest and that is not unreasonable," he replied, keeping his tone carefully even.

Max glanced around the table, his gaze encompassing the humanoid and canine *symbionts* that were gathered. These twelve served as a board of decision making and accountability for the *symbiont* community. History had told them all that they were not above making terrible errors in judgments... errors that had changed world events, many times to the detriment of humanity. This group communicated both telepathically and audibly, and a mixture of soft lupine sounds was interspersed with humanoid voice.

Max spoke again, deliberately keeping his tone light. "Well, I for one am very eager to meet Petra's new companion." His private, unexpressed feeling was envy that Petra was once again in the spotlight. The other telepaths, had they exerted effort, could have perceived this, but this violated their privacy tenants. Max had always been jealous of Petra's genetic ability to travel through time. He was a gifted telepath but he never was able to achieve time travel, no matter the canine pairing. At last his frustration broke to the surface and he stood abruptly.

"Come on, Philo! You know Petra is a loose cannon and has been so for years. We've always had trouble controlling her and Tula." His face darkened as he went on. "That last little stunt of altering an invaluable historic cave painting was just more evidence, another symptom of her recklessness and arrogance." He paused and looked around the table. "She flaunts her travel abilities, she and Tula, knowing that many of us cannot do likewise." Max immediately regretted his last sentence, as it hinted at his true agenda.

Philo picked up on this and remarked, "Max, it is wrong to fault Petra and Tula for natural abilities."

Juno, an aged canine who paralleled Philo in terms of respect bestowed upon her by her peers, inserted her thoughts into the debate.

"Let's all take a moment and remember who we are and why we are here." Her dark brown eyes were bottomless pools of gentleness and vast knowledge. Philo welcomed her counsel above all others.

"We have been through the dark times and have evolved by choice to serve this planet and ultimately humanity." Her thoughts filled all their minds, the flow of which was like a beautifully orchestrated piece of music.

Stone dropped his head, unable to meet her penetrating glance. He actually felt a minor stab of shame; his avarice was potentially consuming, and he had enough self awareness to know this.

"When I was younger and more agile," she continued, "I, too, was a traveler and made my share of mistakes— usually out of naivety—but I usually thought I was doing the right thing. In retrospect, there are many things I would do differently. Is that not the luxury we have as we age? The ability to look back and reexamine our actions with a more experienced eye...." her thoughts trailed off. Juno closed her eyes and her concentration was obvious to the others who politely shared her surface thoughts.

"They are coming," she commented, "Petra and her new companion." Glancing at Philo, she asked, "What do you know of the *symbiont* who travelled here with Petra?"

"Absolutely nothing," he replied, "except what I learned from Petra's thoughts at a distance. And we all know that type of knowledge is flawed and essentially faulty." He gave a faint smile. "But her thoughts were so vivid and strong that they definitely made a distinct impression on me. She obviously finds him completely fascinating; she also has a sense of protectiveness about him, but I'm not sure why just yet. Certainly she didn't feel protective of Tula." After a brief pause, he added, "And there is an oppressive sense of grief over the death of Tula, so let's all remember that here today and try to be kind."

Max stared at a fixed point in the center of the large table. He felt his face flush slightly, since he knew that last comment was directed at him. For all his dislike of Petra, he had appreciated and respected Tula and would miss her.

Juno's head pulled up again, her attitude one of curiosity and anticipation.

"They are on their way." Cocking her head slightly to the right, she added, "As they draw nearer, I can get some measure of her companion." There was a long pause and her eyes gleamed. "I think we are going to be in for a treat."

CHAPTER 6

It was a beautiful late summer day, mild for what was typical this time of year in North Carolina. Kipp and I walked the two miles to Technicorps; I possessed both a car and a bicycle but preferred the walk when the weather was agreeable. The sun was making its elliptical journey and a very slight breeze was stirring my hair about my shoulders. Kipp padded alertly by my side, his nose quivering. His thoughts betrayed his curiosity, and I enjoyed experiencing all that was new from his eyes. To all observers, we just seemed to be a woman and her dog out for a nice stroll. We finally arrived at Technicorps, which was housed in a multistoried compound, nestled in the heart of Research Triangle Park.

Kipp and I entered the institute and, after negotiating a maze of hallways, arrived in the anteroom outside of the conference room where the twelve leaders were congregated. The thoughts of these beings were familiar to me, but of course not to Kipp. He looked at me, needing my leadership in uncertain times.

"You'll be fine," I told him. Having no frame of reference, Kipp really had no concept of his vastly superior capabilities. But he was aware of my total confidence in him.

Philo met us at the door and enfolded me in a much

welcomed embrace. Of course, there was no need for
words as his thoughts flooded through my mind. After a
few moments, he stepped back to gaze at Kipp, who
stood at my side, patient and composed. Philo dropped
down on his knees so that he and Kipp could be at eye
level. Philo closed his eyes and lowered his mental
barriers to let Kipp access his mind. I had allowed Kipp
to have unfettered access to my thoughts, compromising
my comfort level to allow for what would be natural for
Kipp. Part of his adjustment to the modern day would be
to learn self control and respect of others' boundaries.

The rest of the room watched this in fascination, gently
probing and sharing in the experience while maintaining
a polite mental distance. As Kipp and Philo exchanged
thoughts, I monitored the rest of the symbionts, slightly
discomforted by some negative energy, although I
couldn't trace the source. My intuition would lead me to
Max Stone, but I'd been counseled by Philo to exert
some caution in making hasty assumptions in
complicated situations. One of my multitude of faults, I
suppose.

My focus drifted for a moment as my gaze moved
around the large room. I had never liked this room, with
its modern furniture and sterile appearance. My
preference was a more personal feel to any area, hence
my predilection for old furniture, books, odd little jars
and glass bottles found in antique stores. This room had
no personality or uniqueness—just one of thousands of
similar rooms across the country.

After a while, Philo stood up and rubbed his eyes; he
turned to slowly walk to one of the large windows that
faced out into the courtyard with its beautifully
maintained gardens. It was a colorful affair, with late
blooming azaleas and bunches of tall crape myrtles
which had been allowed to grow unfettered. I preferred
them thus, with a dislike of the trimmed variety where
some well meaning soul had attempted a poodle cut, or
whatever it was called. The sun was climbing towards its

zenith and it occurred to me that I had left the cold of a premature winter to be thrown back into late summer. That sort of rapid change in climate had to be making its mark on me, somewhere deep and undetected. Philo interrupted my musing to ask me to join the others at the table. I chose a vacant chair while Kipp took his place at my side on an elevated bench seat, these being provided for the canines present.

"So, Petra, tell us about your journey and how you and Kipp were joined," Philo prompted.

With that invitation, I tried to relay all of my experiences, it always being difficult to compress one's activities that had stretched over a period of two and one half years into a concise recitation. The anthropologists asked their probing questions about the structure of the tribe with whom I'd resided, including the social networks and societal roles; the linguists were curious as to language structure. The *symbionts* trained in zoology were inquisitive about the life forms I encountered and found my story of the cave bear to be amazing; they were mildly skeptical but finally allowed that the story might be factual, given that they could not prove otherwise. Kipp was mildly annoyed that anyone would challenge my veracity—I tried to mentally reassure him that it was not an issue. Later, I would be compelled to meet individually with language experts to record as much of the tribes' language as was possible. This debriefing was extensive and the sun had begun to set on the horizon by the time the group asked about Kipp.

For hours, Kipp remained motionless, his eyes half closed, as he listened to the divergent dialog. He was like a sponge, absorbing information about his new world and these new relationships. I knew Kipp didn't require me to speak for him, so after touching him lightly on his shoulder, I encouraged him to share his history with the group. Concisely, but accurately, he narrated the story of his origin, the memories he had of his mother and her tales of the *symbiont* community of which she had been a member. The group was fascinated and didn't interrupt his narrative. They quickly learned what I knew already: Kipp's mind, the structure of his thoughts, his ability to organize and transmit information was far superior to anyone in the room. Once again, I perceived the faint rumblings of discord, perhaps envy, but in any case something negative. We weren't supposed to push into others thoughts without invitation, so I was cautiously canvassing the group to see if I could locate the source without being accused of being too invasive. Suddenly the atmosphere changed and the mysterious owner of the negativity shut it down, slamming the door on any investigation. He, or she, was good, I thought.

Kipp hadn't missed a beat during all of this and was drawing to the conclusion of his tale, explaining our first symbiotic union and the manner in which it had occurred. He didn't seem tired, but Philo took the opportunity to suggest a break for refreshment. The group agreed and slowly they dispersed; each, prior to leaving the room, came by to meet Kipp and to welcome me back. Juno lingered, speaking softly to Kipp. After a few minutes, she looked at me.

"What an utter delight!" she exclaimed. Juno was as trusted to me as was Philo, so I knew she would be a valuable resource to my beloved Kipp.

I decided to walk out into the garden which had been teasing me from the conference room window. The final days spent in the prehistoric world had left me with a sense that I was still chilled, and the warmth and humidity to be found outside was like an elixir to me. Kipp, naturally, was at my side. The sun rested low in the west and the garden was heavily shadowed. A lichen covered bench in the far corner was a welcomed old friend to me. Seating myself, I watched Kipp move gracefully about the vegetation, looking at plants unknown to him, breathing in unfamiliar scents.

At one point, he looked at me from across the grassy

area and his thoughts were penetrating and distinct: "It was Max."

I didn't need to ask for clarification nor bother to inquire how he knew this. If Kipp stated it, then it was a certainty: the negative influence in the room was Max Stone.

"Kipp, guard your thoughts for now, until we can sort out everything." He grunted softly and I felt his mind close a door in response to my suggestion. He padded back over to me and placed his muzzle on my knees.

"I love you, Petra."

I gently tugged at his upright ears and bent down to rest my cheek on the top of his head. My heart felt suddenly full, and I had to struggle to keep tears from spilling down my cheeks. It was unexpected to me, this intense attachment I had developed for Kipp in such a brief span of time. He saved my life, literally, as well as stepping into the void left by Tula. And he, in return, acted towards me much like a newly hatched foundling duck, imprinting himself on me at first sight. His heart and love were complete, eternally loyal and uncompromising. I felt an intense responsibility to be the best I could be, for Kipp's sake. The sound of a polite throat clearing disturbed my train of thoughts, and I turned to see Philo making his quiet approach.

"Petra, I talked the others into letting you and Kipp go home for the evening and get some rest. I know you are exhausted," he added unnecessarily. "Let me drive you home."

Kipp seemed intrigued, having observed cars during our walk with a mixture of both curiosity and alarm. What should have been a five minute drive home turned into a two hour jaunt into the country. I guess, in some ways, all canines have one thing in common: they love a ride in the car. Kipp stuck his head out the window, his fur parted by the breeze, tongue lolling as his jowls flapped in the wind. Philo and I could not help but laugh at his silly face.

After we had toured Butner, Creedmoor and made a dash through Durham—which involved a brief run through a drive through fast food joint—Philo finally brought us back home. He shut off the car engine, and we sat in the darkness which had fallen, surrounding us in a blanket of solitude.

"Petra, you and Kipp need to take care." Philo said, his voice soft.

Kipp looked from him to me, his thoughts focused on the former attitude of levity that had suddenly taken a serious tone. Philo knew more than he was saying.

"Don't be careful or political with me," I said, suddenly irritated by this covert, nonspecific dialog. I suppose my time with Kipp and his honest, forthright manner had soured me on typical modern discourse. Philo's eyebrows shot up and he gave me a sharp look.

"I am your friend, Petra, so don't you go forgetting that little fact."

Feeling ashamed of my outburst, I looked down at my hands, which were nervously clenched in my lap.

"Sorry, Philo," I began, as he reached over to cover my fists with his large hand.

"No harm done," he replied, smiling at me. "And you're right; I need to be more direct and quit talking in code. Anything said to you needs also to be told to Kipp."

Kipp stuck his head in between us at this point. I put my arm around his neck and pulled his face to mine.

"Petra," he said, "I don't need you to protect me." He paused to collect his thoughts and continued his dialog. "I was living in a savage land before coming here, and I'm not a child."

"No, you aren't, but you lack knowledge of modern technology, and I just don't want anyone to try and take advantage of you."

Kipp started to reply, but Philo cut him off.

"Kipp, there are issues here that have serious implications. It is not that you aren't bright enough or perceptive enough to weed your way through the obstacle course, but you will need someone to be your guard." He looked at me. "And there is no one more capable than Petra that can do that for you." Philo was quiet for a moment before laughing softly. "There is a current slang expression that will suffice here, Kipp: Petra 'has your back'."

Kipp's reply was to lick the side of my face. We bade Philo good bye and retired to the seclusion of my little house. Exhausted to the core, we had a small meal and collapsed into bed. There would be more long days to follow.

CHAPTER 7

Peter rushed along the dimly lit passage in the subbasement of the Technicorps office complex. If he were late one more time, he fretted, Fitzhugh would have his head on a silver platter. Finally he reached the door to the library, which was hidden far beneath the imposing corporate structure that rested above. Of course, Fitzhugh would have it no other way; he wanted a dark, secretive cavern in which to work. He was too much a creature of his past and needed less sterile surroundings for his creativity to flow.

Cautiously opening the door, Peter hoped for a moment that perhaps the old man was occupied and would not take notice of his tardiness. That hope was short lived when he heard the familiar, raspy voice call out from behind a stack of books which lined a corridor to his left. The apparition of Fitzhugh soon followed his voice, and Peter looked up at the tall, spare man. Unfortunately for Peter, the wizened face wore a scowl; his lateness had been suitably noted and documented, no doubt.

Turning away without a word, Fitzhugh led Peter to the work station which was hidden in a maze of stacked documents, manuals, periodicals, maps and other papers which dated back several hundred years. They could have had any number of well lit, cheerful and modern office spaces with tiny cubicles and furniture made of compressed particle board, but Fitzhugh always preferred an area that smacked of ancient times. His one concession, however, to the present, was a sophisticated computer which rested on a desk that he had acquired in England some 900 years earlier, when he was a comparatively young lad. A librarian, scholar, and chronicler of history, he was even then; an aberrant, he avoided the traveling which seemed so seductive to all other *symbionts*. Funny, but now the ability to travel through time seemed restricted to such a small number. He did not understand the science behind it all; he just was working to complete the historical records before his time came to an end. And close it was—he could feel the shadows of death pressing about him even now. Not many *symbionts* lived to the age of 1378.

Fitzhugh's fascination with history and the accurate recording of such began when he was quite young, and at that time in his life he did join with a *symbiont* in order to travel. Always, his preferred destination was the ancient library in Alexandria. Spending countless hours among the manuscripts, he read of Socrates and Aristotle; all the ancient musings filled his mind and impressed upon him the need to maintain an accurate historical record. The truth of this was pressed home when the library, with its invaluable and irreplaceable cargo, was destroyed by fire. When his *symbiont* subsequently died of an unexpected illness, Fitzhugh decided to forgo all traveling and dedicated his life to recording the history of the *symbiont* species.

Peter took his place before the computer and tapped his feet restlessly as he waited for it to boot up. Fitzhugh gave a deep sigh; these youngsters had not learned the value of patience, an acquired skill in a species that lived to vastly advanced years in comparison to all other earthly beings. They would be using a program that would allow the computer to scan documents written in the *symbiont* language, index these documents and then allow for them to be translated into any of 130 known languages. As the keeper of all the documents in existence, Fitzhugh was hurrying to make certain this project was complete. One never knew how much sand remained in the hourglass.

"Alright, young one," he began, his soft voice interrupting Peter's chaotic thoughts, "it is time to focus. We are about to begin reviewing the story of the Mayan people and Donnelle's involvement with that culture." He walked down a long corridor and, after examining a stack of binders, found the one he needed. The temperature and humidity in the library were controlled to help preserve the ancient manuscripts, but even so there was deterioration. Returning to the desk, Fitzhugh opened the binder with care and removed the desired documents. A musty odor wafted up and Peter suppressed the need to sneeze. To Fitzhugh, the smell was almost like an aphrodisiac; he half closed his eyes in pleasure.

Peter began to scan the story, which had been told to Fitzhugh by the lupine *symbiont*, Tiobe, shortly before his death in the year 1275. Since this was a first hand account, it was considered to be a reliable record.

Donnelle the Elder, 1103, AD

In the year 1103, Donnelle the Elder traveled to the year 853 AD, to the historic lands of the Mayan civilization. Having spread their culture and advancements throughout Mesoamerica, the results were expansive and progressive development of widespread cities and imposing structures and influence over multitudes of people. Donnelle the Elder was a historian and sociologist, and he and his *symbiont*, Tiobe, specialized in cultural observations to document the effects of an autocratic ruling class on the development of the people subject to their rule.

Donnelle was an ethical historian and always resisted the temptation of involvement in cultures he investigated, but he had aged, and in this his 758th year, he had become weary after countless years of observation of people suffering under oppression. Even in cultures which thrived, he mourned for the majority of the people who toiled endlessly under the rule of a few; the peasants, the workers—the ones who were to achieve little in life—theirs was a life of endless and exhausting toil in an effort to survive from day to day.

Donnelle and Tiobe traveled to visit the Mayan civilization in a place later known as Piedro Negros. As he had done many times before, Donnelle carefully inserted himself in the culture, observing it for many years and carefully crafting a role for himself. Unknown to Tiobe, Donnelle had made a decision which violated the very concept of the *symbiont* as a neutral observer: no longer would he be passive and inert. Donnelle wanted to improve the lives of the peasant class. Tiobe, his *symbiont*, should have discerned these thoughts, but Donnelle took care to conceal his true agenda. Later, it would be too late for Tiobe to stop him.

Donnelle made certain the ruling class at Piedro Negros noticed his intelligence and capabilities. Due to his telepathic gifts, he could make pronouncements that to the ancient Mayans seemed divinely inspired. Eventually, he became a shaman, a valued advisor to the king. As have many who overvalue their contributions to any people, he became deluded over his role and his perceived abilities to convert the society to a more democratic one.

Over time, and gradually, Donnelle became an important figure in the structure of the Mayan civilization, and Tiobe was dismayed to find his once balancing influence over his partner had diminished. Tiobe was to watch all that unfolded from a position of complete powerlessness. Donnelle used his telepathy to learn that the king was fearful that one day the land would no longer support his growing empire. Whether or not the gods smiled upon the land with a good harvest and bountiful rains was not within his control, no matter how pious he might be. Donnelle subsequently used his knowledge of the king's anxieties to plant a seed: he advised the king that his reading of the spirit world indicated that there would be a prolonged drought and that his people would suffer and revolt against his rule. He and all his family would be destroyed in the resulting chaos.

The king, not so much to preserve the lives of his people, but to assure his own survival and his wealth, sent the people from the cities; they were dispersed throughout the territory so that they might make the land fruitful and able to support small tribes rather than a huge city. Word of the impending drought spread throughout the Mayan nation and the other kings followed what had taken place at Piedro Negros. Ultimately, the once great Mayan cities would languish and fall into ruin, all due to a drought that never occurred—the outcome of the calculated influence of a misguided *symbiont* who viewed himself as the savior of the poor people.

Donnelle the Elder finally returned to his century to face the disapprobation of his peers. The others separated him from Tiobe and his days of traveling came to a sudden end.

Donnelle died at the age of 891, his broken spirit apparent to all. Upon his death bed, his old friend and companion, Tiobe, was allowed to visit him one last time and they once again merged their thoughts in familiar companionship. This brought comfort to the old man whose light life was almost extinguished. Donnelle asked for forgiveness for having brought the shadow of deception and shame to Tiobe.

Fitzhugh sat quietly, in reflection, recalling with crisp accuracy the day when Tiobe had shared the history with him. Peter knew him well enough by now to give him time to process the memories. Peter gently probed Fitzhugh's mind and felt he could safely pose a question.

"Master," he began with deference, "I don't understand

the significance of this story. Why would anyone need to know what happened that long ago?"

Fitzhugh gave him a withering glance. The young ones had no respect for history.

"Peter, I have told you before: we need knowledge of history so that we can learn from mistakes and hopefully evolve to make better choices."

"But Master," Peter persisted, "look at humans. They engage in wars, over and over again, and always about the same issues: power, wealth, control and acquisition. Their knowledge of history does not seem to keep them from making war on one another. No matter what, they seem to teeter on the edge of self destruction."

"We are not human, Peter." Fitzhugh had to state the obvious. "And our abilities have given us the power to change history and alter civilizations; therefore, we must learn from our mistakes." He paused for a moment, fatigue had overtaken him, and he took a seat in his comfortable, overstuffed chair that was angled near the workstation. Changing the subject, he said, "Peter, I understand we are to expect some visitors and I think you will find the entire experience to be an exciting one." Peter's eyes widened and Fitzhugh could feel the pulsing of his curious thoughts.

"Tell me more, Master, please."

Fitzhugh gave him a thin smile in response. "You will have to wait, as will I, to learn more." Fitzhugh slowly stretched his frame from his chair and, picking up the manuscript, walked slowly down the corridor to return it to its previous resting place. He turned back to glance at Peter. "But for now, young one, we must continue with our work."

Peter gave a small sigh but knew not to speak. Anyone who achieved the seniority of Fitzhugh did not care to hear a mere child's complaints over being tired due to too much work.

CHAPTER 8

Kipp awakened me at an early hour, eager to eat and go for a run. The day or two we had spent in relative inactivity was grating on him, accustomed as he was to a very high activity level. Kipp, I reminded myself, was a hunter and had spent his life in the aggressive pursuit of survival. Staggering out of bed, I managed to pull together a small breakfast for us. The cupboards were low and I was going to have to make a grocery bill soon, lest Kipp start hunting the neighborhood for game. That had the potential of making us both very unpopular.

We finished eating, and I located some worn sweats; after stretching, we took off, inhaling deep breaths of the early morning air, which held just a touch of coolness. I probably was in the best physical shape of my life during my time with the prehistoric tribe but had become seriously weakened during the last few weeks prior to our fortuitous return home. Kipp wanted to run, but about all I could manage was a moderately rapid walk. There were few cars, so I let Kipp off his lead so that he could really stretch out. There was no worry, since he and I were in constant mental contact.

We arrived at a large vacant field which lay on the edge of a woods and he raced off, moving with sheer delight, barking, darting, and leaping as he flew over the long grass. At one point, he was about 50 yards ahead of me, and he turned, facing me, the wind ruffling his dense fur coat. His mind projected intense pleasure at this freedom and his reconnection with nature.

Suddenly, his mind changed focus and he turned to stare intently at something close by in the tall grass. I trotted up to his location and found him standing tensely, his nose down close to the ground, a posture of curiosity and caution. There was a tiny disturbance in the grass, and I stooped down to gently part it with my hands. There, in a little puff of tabby striped fur, was a tiny kitten, mewling softly. The kitten took one look at Kipp and commenced with a defensive posture, arched back, hair on end, and enough hissing to make a king cobra proud. Kipp, startled, hopped back about a yard. I could not help but laugh and Kipp looked slightly miffed.

"What on earth is that little creature, all teeth and claws?" he asked.

"That's a domestic cat, a young one, something we call a kitten. She is the domesticated version of a creature you would be familiar with: our old friend the cave lion."

"You must be joking," Kipp replied, rolling his eyes at me.

"No, but what worries me is that one this young wouldn't normally be off by herself."

I instructed Kipp to make several forays and use his superior nose to look for a mother and litter mates. After about an hour of making increasingly large circles, Kipp returned to give me the bad news—the kitten had probably been abandoned, tossed nearby by someone who was too irresponsible to try and find her a home. I explained my surmise to him, and he lowered his head in disgust; the behaviors of humans were foreign to his code of ethics. Before I could go any further, Kipp went over to the still spitting tiny tiger and, braving her swats on his sensitive nose, gently picked her up in his mouth and began to trot towards home, me lagging behind.

"I admire her bravery, so we won't leave her to despair," he said. "Her mind is all instinct and fear," he added, "but soon she'll learn we mean her no harm."

I was fascinated but not surprised at this point by anything the noble Kipp would do.

"Can you communicate with her at all?" I asked, not certain, but knowing I couldn't.

He gave an uncharacteristic pause before responding, and I had the distinct impression he was being careful in his reply.

"To a limited degree I can reassure her and let her know she is safe. I also can assure her that her empty belly will soon be full. She likes that idea the best."

I took a deep breath as we drew near home. Kipp had taken charge of this situation, so if he wanted to be nursemaid to a baby, it was alright with me.

"She needs a name," I commented. "Any ideas?" I asked Kipp.

He considered for a moment and then queried, "What's the name of that pretty flower in the garden, the one I admired yesterday?" I accessed his thoughts and saw the picture of a rosy hued day lily.

I told him and he exclaimed, "That's it! We'll call her Lily."

We arrived home, and I kept my fingers crossed that Lily was weaned and could eat solid food. She was small, but her eyes no longer had the cloudy, unfocused blue of a very young kitten. I put out the last of the canned chicken and Lily proceeded to eat until she almost collapsed as her belly grew round and full. Kipp had taken up guard next to her, perched on his haunches like an animated Sphinx. I left them to prepare for the upcoming day, which promised to be a long one.

In a short time, we left for Technicorps. I knew what Kipp did not: the medical team would want to do a physical exam on me as well as Kipp, who would not be happy, I predicted. We took Lily along, too. One of the veterinarians could check her out while Kipp was being examined. Lily at this point had stopped hissing at Kipp, who carried her in his mouth.

As we walked along, I took time, anew, to appreciate the beauty of the small town and the surrounding territory. This area of the piedmont was picture perfect, with gently sloping hills, abundant trees and colorful foliage. The sky above was a limitless blue; indeed, the color seemed to stretch forever into space. A few onlookers looked with startled glances at the duo of Kipp and Lily; I would have to buy some sort of carrier for her, I reminded myself, before someone called the police to report me for animal abuse of a kitten.

At Technicorps, we once again went to the board room where the group of Twelve was in conference. I was grateful to learn their interest was in Kipp—I was in the comfortable secondary spot –so I exited to take Lily downstairs to the animal health research division. One of the veterinarians was well known to me, having ministered often to Tula. He was the sole *symbiont* in his division, leading a team of humans.

"Well, hello, Petra. It's been a long time." Tom Hughes met me, a broad smile on his face. He, of course, knew about Tula and his thoughts betrayed his intense sorrow; she had been a good friend to him and his family.

"What have you here?" he asked, looking at the tabby fur ball I was holding.

"Kipp found her this morning." I didn't need to explain about Kipp, since the news of my return in concert with a novice *symbiont* from ancient times had run through our small community like wildfire. "Can you check her out and see if she is healthy?" I added, "She's really small but was able to eat some solid food this morning."

Tom scratched Lily's tiny chin with his forefinger and she rotated her head to maximize the caress.

"She's a pretty little thing." Pausing, he looked over his shoulder and called to one of the technicians to take Lily and prepare her for some laboratory tests as well as an exam.

"I look forward to meeting Kipp later on today," he added.

I had put it off as long as possible, but it was my scheduled time to see the physician, too. Dragging along slowly, I finally made it to the suite of offices and signed in as directed by the cheerful receptionist, who looked at me over her half glasses.

"Good morning, Ms. Goodgame," she piped up, her voice pleasant and suspiciously happy in tone. Surely my arrival had not brought her such boundless joy. She was obviously more pleased to be here than was I.

After a short wait, the nurse directed me to the examination room and I waited, not patiently, for Dr. Mills. He finally burst in, his booming voice just a small indication of his nature. A short, round faced man, he perpetually seemed to be in a good mood, the ebullience of which was occasionally annoying to his less than enthusiastic patients. In fact, as I thought about it, everyone in this office was irritatingly nice.

"Hello, Petra," he greeted me, before seating himself on a little round stool on wheels, his ample backside hanging over the narrow margins of the seat.

At the completion of a journey, the job of the physician was to complete a total assessment, including physical and mental. I dreaded the inevitable talk about Tula, but knew I would have to give him all the painful details if I ever wanted to get out of this room. After completing his examination, he asked me to come to his office after getting dressed.

"Close the door and have a seat," he said. "Coffee?"

"Yes, thanks, that would be nice." I watched as he prepared the beverage, filling half his mug with cream and six teaspoons of sugar before adding a splash of steaming coffee. Knowing my preference, he left my mug unaltered.

"Petra, physically I think you seem basically okay, a testament to your solid constitution. But you're depleted, and your story indicates you've had several weeks of starvation level existence. I'll give you dietary suggestions for refeeding, as well as some supplements that are recommended. You'll need to avoid any vigorous physical activity for the next month and then gradually work back to your previous level of exercise tolerance." He paused for a moment.

"As to your psychological state, I have some concerns that you haven't had the opportunity to grieve over the loss of Tula. Losing one's *symbiont* is the most catastrophic lost that can occur to one of us, and I fear you've mustered too much of the 'be strong and tough it out' mentality. I can schedule you some time with a therapist, if you'd like."

We stared at each other for a moment, and he could already read my response which was decidedly negative.

"I know what to do; I just have to do it." I paused, faltering, before adding, "I have had serious loss before, and I dealt with that, if you recall."

"Well, maybe you did; time will tell."

I was getting annoyed at this point.

"I don't need a therapist to tell me that I have grief and try and explain the stages of loss to me and figure out where I'm at in the process. If you need to know, I'm still working on the guilt part and will let you know how it proceeds." While my proficient and nimble use of sarcasm was one of my greatest skills, it also posed one of my most profound liabilities.

"And, it seems, you're still working on your anger, too," he replied, his voice soft. "Let me know if you need anything." He crossed the room to give me a shoulder squeeze before setting me free.

I decided to use my time wisely, and, after asking Tom Hughes if I could borrow his car, I drove to a nearby market and purchased some groceries. I also ran by a pet store to pick up some cat food, bowls and a carrier for Lily. Driving to the house, I quickly deposited the food items and returned to Technicorps. Soon, I was waiting in the anteroom outside the conference room where I had left Kipp. So much for rest and building up my exercise tolerance! There was a disturbance inside, and as I prepared to focus on the discordant thoughts, the door flew open and Philo walked out, agitated, his hands ruffling through his unkempt hair.

"Petra, it's time for Kipp to go downstairs and let Tom check him out medically."

"What's happened, Philo?" I asked, alarmed by his presentation.

He darted a quick look at me, his face dark with congested blood, before glancing back over his shoulder where the others were congregated. His eyes met Max's and his thoughts suddenly shuttered.

"I'll have to talk with you at another time," he replied.

Kipp sauntered out to join me, a confident snap in his stride, and I knew that whatever had happened had not disturbed his solid sense of self.

"Where's Lily?" he asked.

After telling him, I added that he shared the same fate—a physical exam by Dr Hughes. He wasn't very happy but apparently had decided which battles to choose, and this wasn't one of them. We completed the rest of the day in relative peace. Kipp and Lily both survived the veterinarian and were proclaimed healthy.

We arrived home and Kipp took over the care of Lily. Due to his ability to decode her primitive mind, he knew when she was hungry, as well as when she needed to take care of her elimination needs. He no longer had to pick her up in his mouth to carry her outside—she had learned to follow him like a baby duck putters along in the wake of its mother. That evening, when we got ready to retire, Kipp crawled up on the bed next to me, Lily on board for the ride. He curled up, his body touching mine, while Lily reclined upon his neck.

"Petra, I'm not sure what happened today, because I don't understand the technology." He paused for a moment and nuzzled Lily, who was batting at his nose in a playful moment.

"Philo was very upset, especially at Max Stone, who was wanting ...." his thoughts trailed off, suddenly distracted by Lily. He had been thwarted by an occurrence he could not process: Lily, who had settled in for the evening, began to purr.

"What on earth is that noise?" he asked, a mental frown wrinkling his normally calm brow.

"Well, Kipp, if you can figure that one out, you'll accomplish much. The last I heard, learned scientists were still pondering the mystery of the purr." I paused before asking, "When you try to access her little brain, what do you make of it?"

Kipp concentrated for a moment before giving a reply. "She's all feeling, this little one. She's happy her belly is full; she is warm and she feels, well, safe. But I admit I'm alarmed to say, she thinks I'm her mother."

I ruffled his ears and gave Lily a scratch on her head. Of course, as is predictable with a kitten, she grabbed my hand, bit it, and then kicked it several times with her hind legs to make certain she had killed the big hand.

"Okay, Kipp, now that you have let Lily distract you, let's get back to your story about meeting with the *symbiont* group today."

Kipp adjusted himself on the bed for a moment, trying to get comfortable with Lily still cavorting on his neck.

"Philo got upset with Max, who was talking about something I don't understand. All I know is that Philo reacted severely, thinking the discussion was inappropriate and frankly immoral."

"What word was Max using, Kipp?"

He concentrated for a moment.

"Cloning, I think it was called. What is that, Petra?"

I stared at him for a moment, taking in his profile as he gently nuzzled Lily in a failed attempt to make her be still and settled. Why on earth would Max have been discussing cloning at a meeting featuring Kipp? I quickly became alarmed, and before Kipp could say more, I had dialed Philo. As I waited impatiently for him to answer, it felt as if time had slowed; I could hear the clock ticking loudly and from outside could even hear the cicadas making their music. For a moment it felt as if my senses were amplified, and I could hear the blood rushing in my ears. A few seconds later, Philo's voice boomed in my ear; it was clear I had awakened him.

"Couldn't this have waited until morning," he started, recognizing my number. We'd known each other long enough to skip some of the niceties. Feeling combative, I didn't bother to apologize for the time of day.

"No, it couldn't. I'd like an explanation as to why Max and the Twelve were having a discussion on cloning?" I demanded.

The line went quiet, and for a flash I wondered if he had hung up. By this time, Kipp was watching me intently, his eyes focused, and I could feel his concern, not for himself, but for me.

"Petra, you have always trusted me," Philo said, his voice steady. "So you must trust me now."

I felt like I was navigating the ocean without a sextant, unable to use my abilities to read Philo's thoughts and discern his feeling tone. In an instant, I was embarrassed that I had even nurtured such a thought of suspicion. This was Philo, after all, my closest friend.

Chagrined, I replied, "I do trust you, I just don't understand why you didn't tell me what was going on."

"Max thinks we should investigate cloning Kipp, since he is such a genetically unique individual; basically his kind is extinct for all intents and purposes. While the rest of the *symbiont* population has been altered through genetic degradation, Kipp is still, well, the genuine article." Philo paused for a moment as he gathered his thoughts. "But you should know that he only had the minimal support of two others; the plan was soundly voted down."

"Well, I don't trust Max at all, so I do plan to make certain Kipp is protected, Philo. You can depend on that."

Philo concurred and added, "And you can depend on me and Juno to do the same".

Before he rung off, Philo suggested we meet at Duke Forrest early the next morning for a long walk so that we could talk more. I agreed and hung up.

"Petra, what's going on?" Kipp asked. He moved a little closer to me on the bed, careful to not disturb the now slumbering Lily, who was stretched across his flank.

I was tired; my adrenaline burst had fatigued me. Asking him to postpone the discussion until morning, I turned off the lights, submerging us in a cocoon of darkness. Sleep overtook us, and I welcomed it.

CHAPTER 9

I fell into a restless sleep, the type of night where one is buffeted by a cascade of dreams; some were teasingly good, while others were bad in a way that left lingering anxiety long after awakening. My current dream had evolved into a terrible nightmare, something I had rarely experienced in my life, never having been subject to such. In my dream, Kipp and I had traveled through time to ancient Egypt, where we appeared inside the temple at Luxor. Of course, by our simple presence, we had violated a sacred place, and the startled priests pursued us with deadly intent, as did the temple guardians.

We raced through dimly lit corridors, the magnificent architecture and sculptures lost to my examination in our haste. I fell behind the fleet Kipp, who slowed his pace to allow me to catch up. Screaming at him, I urged him to run—run for his life—but he kept looking over his shoulder at me. No matter what I tried to do, I could not elude the pursuing guards, nor could I make Kipp abandon me to save himself.

Gathering myself, I tried to run faster but only managed to twist my ankle when I took a bad step; the momentary lag allowed the man who had drawn closest to me to grab my arm. He was huge, very strong, and he yanked me to a sudden stop, the interrupted momentum snapping my neck with ferocity. Pulling me close to him with his one hand which completely encircled my upper arm, he began to drag me back into the depths of the temple, as I struggled helplessly to free myself. With preternatural instinct he turned to look over my shoulder, eyes widening in terror. I could almost see the reflection of Kipp in his dark eyes, as Kipp launched himself at the man, knocking him down with a blow to the chest.

Reading Kipp's thoughts, I knew he had no intention of harming the man; he was just trying to give me an opportunity to escape. One of the man's companions, who had closed within striking range, launched a spear which, to my eye, appeared to move in slow motion towards Kipp. My mouth opened in a soundless scream....

It was at that moment, my dream began to change. Even though I was sleeping, I had some sense that it was oddly different, that it was not progressing as it should. The spear, which was whistling through the air, turned into dust and fell to the floor. The pursuing guards stopped running towards us and stood still momentarily before sitting quietly on the floor, their eyes downward cast. Kipp returned to my side, leaving the prone guard uninjured on the floor.

"Let's go, Petra," he said, beckoning me to follow him. As I looked at him, his eyes were bright, his tail gently waving its plumed crest. Even though the temple was semi dark, all of the rust toned hues of his coat were rippling with reflected light. There was a hypnotic quality to him—eyes, which glowed in the dim light, drew me to obey his command.

I suddenly awoke, sitting up in bed with a gasp. The room was engulfed in darkness, the soft buzz of a fan comforting me with its white noise. Reaching my hand out, I found Kipp and lightly caressed his head—he was awake. The gentle, familiar touch of his mind was there, entangled with mine.

"Kipp, what was that?" I asked, not sure what had

happened. In my 400 plus years of life, I had never had an experience like that and quite frankly it was very unsettling.

Kipp lay silent and still as he gathered his thoughts.

"My mother told me to not do it or at least to not let anyone know I was doing it...." his thoughts trailed off.

"What exactly did you do?"

I turned on my side and propped myself up on an elbow so that I was facing Kipp. The room was dark, but I could visualize his outline, backlit by glimmers of ambient light which peeked through gaps in the window blinds.

"Well, I was awakened by your dream; it was making you unhappy, so I changed it so that you wouldn't be so distressed." Kipp yawned and casually licked his forepaw.

The import of what he said hit me like a tsunami! Kipp not only was a talented telepath, but also he had the ability to insert thoughts into someone else's mind. As far as I knew, this was an unheard of ability in the symbiotic species. This made Kipp even more unique, more valued, and potentially more dangerous and destabilizing to our small community.

"Did I do something wrong, Petra?" he asked, now worried that he had upset me.

"No, Kipp, you didn't. It's never wrong to utilize a natural talent. It's just that this ability of yours is very unusual, and I've never known anyone that can do what you just did." After pausing, I asked, "Why did your mother tell you to not use your ability to change others thoughts?"

Lily began to stir; we both could hear her soft rumbling purrs as she began to knead Kipp's rufous fur. Happiness and contentment emanated from her, and one did not have to be a *symbiont* to decipher it.

"My mother, when she recognized what I could do, told me that only a very few of us—and only lupine symbionts—could influence the thinking of others. She told me that my father had that ability, so she believed it came from him to me."

Kipp paused for a moment to gently nuzzle the top of Lily's little head. "She said the humanoid *symbionts* were threatened by this ability that they did not share, so my father and others in his family had learned to conceal it so that there would be no disruption in harmony." He moved closer to me and placed his muzzle on my chest. "I just didn't want you to hurt—in your dream, I mean."

I lay there for a while, mulling over what I had learned and trying to consider what to do in response. Kipp lay next to me, quiet, patient, waiting for me to take the lead. His trust in me was complete and as a result, I felt an immense responsibility to do the right thing, at least where he was concerned. Was he influencing me to make better choices I wondered, in that moment? It was a question that humans posed from time to time. Does being in the presence of good influence others to act for the common good? I was no philosopher, so I would leave this psychic struggle for another time. Kipp was gently grooming Lily, giving her a sloppy little cowlick. Lily wore a look of complete disgust and tried to elude him, but he had pinned her with a paw and was determined to complete her ablutions.

"Kipp, I really trust Philo. I'd like to tell him about all of this and let him advise us both. But short of that, I don't want you to tell anyone about your, well, special talents. Okay?"

"Sure, Petra, whatever you think is best."

It was only five AM, but I knew further sleep would elude me. Kipp was encouraged to take Lily out for her morning constitutional, while I worked on an early breakfast. Soon the coffee was going, and I sat back to enjoy the coming dawn, a time of day I had always treasured. There was something about that moment, when the still of dark night gave way to the sky's slow and reluctant illumination by the sun, which was lurking from somewhere beneath the horizon; tongues of color darted across the blue black palette and the early awakened birds welcomed the impending change with their varied cries. I took my coffee out to the small garden in the rear of my house and joined Kipp and Lily as they explored the grass, shrubs, flowers and trees. There was a slight breeze that cooled my heated skin. For a brief moment, I wished that life were simple and that I did not have to feel so responsible for Kipp's development. But then shame flooded me, as I recalled all the blessings I had experienced in my life. All creatures had challenges, and existence was not intended to be an effortless parade. Kipp glanced at me, amused, as he watched Lily tackling her predatory challenge: the pursuit of a rather large garden spider.

We stayed thus, enjoying wordless companionship amidst the breaking of dawn. It was just a short time later that Philo arrived, and off we went on our journey to Duke Forest. Kipp insisted on bringing Lily along, much to Philo's disapproval. There we were, an odd quartet, zipping along in Philo's ancient and battered Honda Civic. At Kipp's urging, I rolled down the passenger window and he stuck his head out, letting the wind flatten his ears and tangle his coat. Lily, finding the breeze a bit too much for her liking, made her way to my lap and actually settled down, a rare occurrence for her. Philo was well known for his tendency to break all speed limits as well as a number of other traffic laws. At one point, as we careened around a sharp curve, Kipp lost his happy face as he scrambled desperately to regain his footing.

"Sorry about that," Philo muttered, glancing at Kipp's accusatory expression staring back at him in the rearview mirror. He eased off the accelerator a little, but I could tell that Kipp was going to wait a while before regaining his trust in the driver.

We covered the distance in a brief time and parked; only one other car was present. This pleased me, since I preferred a quiet, isolated walk. It was still rather dimly lit here on the edge of the forest, but the rays of first light were beginning to dart through the tree limbs and heavy forestation; the mist was being burned off, rising from the ground to create a slight fog that lingered in wisps and banks. Kipp ran ahead, followed by the bouncing Lily who was working to keep him in sight.

Philo, hair mussed, eyes darkened from lack of sleep, ambled along in silence. I knew him well enough to recognize his sleep deprivation was due to his concerns over what was going on at Technicorps in terms of Kipp. Despite all his reassurances, he, too, had some worries.

"Petra," he began, "you don't have to fret about Kipp. I'll make certain that he's not, well, misused by anyone at Technicorps—including Max."

I brushed away his words as if batting away flies.

"Philo, that's not what concerns me now. Something else has happened, something I need to tell you about...." my voice trailed off.

"You're afraid!" he exclaimed, taking me gently by the arm and turning me to face him.

Instead of answering him, I called out for Kipp to return. In a short time, he bounded up, followed by the now fatigued Lily. His tail was gently waving, his face split by a huge dog type smile, tongue lolling.

"Kipp, I want you to demonstrate for Philo what you were showing me last night." I paused for a moment before adding, "And, Philo, I want you to focus in on Kipp's mind; forget politeness and our customary reserve, you need to monitor Kipp's thoughts."

Philo frowned at me, probably suspecting I was trying to play some sort of trick on him. But he turned to Kipp and took an attentive stance. As we stood there, Lily stopped her wanderings, suddenly turned, and raced towards us, tail scimitar curved, hair on end —the run terminated when she climbed my jean clad leg as if it were a telephone pole.

"Ouch!" I exclaimed. "Was that necessary, Kipp?"

He laughed in response. As I leaned forward to

massage my leg and pluck off the clinging Lily, Philo looked at me, his face suddenly pale.

"Can one of you tell me what just happened?"

Trying to cradle the struggling Lily, I finally let her hop down.

"Philo, I think you know what happened: Kipp caused Lily to run at me like that by planting certain thoughts in her mind."

Kipp was looking at one and then the other of us.

"What thought did you, well, inject into Lily?" Philo asked him.

"I made her think there was an animal after her, causing her to run for safety," Kipp responded. After pausing for a moment, he sheepishly added, "I let her think you were a tree, Petra."

Philo asked, "Are you telling me that you can plant your thoughts in other beings, making them act in a certain way, thinking these thoughts to be of their making?"

Both Kipp and I replied in the affirmative, and I shared the dream experience of early that morning. Kipp went on to divulge his knowledge of his paternal family and this rather rare skill. Philo was astonished as I had been, having never heard of any *symbiont* with this ability. He was in agreement with me that we should deal with this new wrinkle carefully.

"Kipp, if it is all the same to you, I'd prefer we only share this information with Juno and Fitzhugh," Philo said.

"Why Fitzhugh?" I queried, curious as to Philo's choices. "I mean, Juno makes sense, and I trust her implicitly. But Fitzhugh?"

"Fitzhugh is the keeper of our history; if anyone living knows of this, it would be he. And while I realize that you and he have had certain, well, brush ups in the past, I find him to be completely trustworthy."

Kipp gave his consent so that Philo might share. After that, he wandered off to collect Lily, who was still in the afterglow of having been treed on my leg by her imaginary pursuer. Philo and I walked slowly, each deep in our own thoughts.

At one point, Philo surprised me by offering, "You realize, don't you, that you don't have to question yourself so much."

"What do you mean?" I asked.

"You're the only one who fears you lack the ability to make the right choices. We all have an Achilles' heel, and that's yours." He added, "I have always found you to be well grounded, centered and ethical. This is why Tula's death impacted you as it did, even though you won't talk about it; you will never allow that perhaps you couldn't have changed the outcome, no matter what you might have done. Sometimes things just happen. The fact you could not alter her destiny does not imply you did something wrong or even that you failed to act. I think what I'm trying to tell you is that you need to have more confidence. Perhaps Kipp is here for a reason, as far as you are concerned."

With effort, I avoided making a sarcastic comment along the line that I was unaware that he was a believer in predestination. My attempts to distance him and deflect his comments would only annoy him and I would be so transparent as to seem ridiculous. Telepaths had few secrets and that could be both good and bad, I had found.

The remainder of the walk back to the car was made in silence. The zephyr-like Lily more than ever earned my admiration at her effortless existence. We were due to be back at Technicorps by mid morning. Both Philo and I would have to use our skills of discipline to contain our thoughts in regards to Kipp.

CHAPTER 10

By late morning we were back at Technicorps. The amount of debriefing following a time journey was always astounding, but this was compounded even more since Kipp had entered into the equation. I was scheduled to meet with the linguists to begin the exhaustive process of examining and documenting the early tribe's language, such as it was. Kipp, on the other hand, would spend much of the day with the twelve leaders. I didn't envy Philo the task of keeping his knowledge of Kipp's special ability tucked deeply away in his mind. Certainly, I wouldn't want Max to learn of it, lest he find even more reasons to want to utilize Kipp as if he were a marketable commodity.

This day seemed particularly long and arduous, and I was somewhere beyond fatigue when told that I was released for the day. Walking out to the garden, I waited for Kipp while sitting in the shade of an enormous yellow poplar. In my youth, I had referred to it by its common name—tulip poplar—before being corrected by an elder who had no sense of humor. But in any case, the tree's tulip shaped flowers which appeared each spring were unique and lovely. Before too long, Philo, Kipp, and the ever present Lily joined me. I had only thought I was going home, but Philo had other plans.

"Petra, I've arranged for you, me, and Kipp to meet with Juno and Fitzhugh this evening after everyone else has gone for the day. We need privacy for discussion and research." Philo went on to share that he had briefed Juno on the new revelations regarding Kipp. Much to his surprise, Juno was not unfamiliar with this but had always regarded such as myth versus reality.

Thus, it was a few hours later, after darkness had fallen and Technicorps was functionally closed for business, that we found ourselves in Fitzhugh's lair, the towering archival stacks lending to the cozy atmosphere of antiquity. He had long since sent his assistant home for the day, having been cautioned by Philo as to the need for privacy. I had always found Fitzhugh fascinating although rather intimidating due to his chronic disapproval of me; I think he believed me to be a sloppy historian, certainly not up to his rigid standards. He gave little of himself away to anyone and was so passionately involved in his work that he generally was uninterested in the machinations of the rest of us. Not knowing him well, I was interested to note that he immediately took to Lily and she to him. She had hopped on his desk, a profoundly out of bounds area for all of us, but he smiled indulgently and caressed her when she climbed in his lap and, after making a few circles, settled down.

Fitzhugh hadn't met Kipp but had heard rumors of him from the gossip shared by his apprentice. From Kipp's perspective, he would accept Lily's behavior as a tacit endorsement of the ancient historian. Fitzhugh gave me a curt nod and the irritation directed at me was discernible to all present. He obviously had not forgotten my previous escapade some 200 years earlier when I had, in a silly moment while under the influence of some fermented honey based beverage, altered a hieroglyphic by drawing a little mustache on the face of a female figure during a trip to ancient Egypt. It had been a high spirited action by a young and self indulgent *symbiont*.

Philo cleared his voice and began. "Fitzhugh, I've had

some information shared with me, the nature of which is highly confidential." He paused and waited for Fitzhugh's permission to continue. At his nod, Philo asked, "Do you have any knowledge, historically, of *symbionts* with the ability to transmit and insert thoughts into other beings? This, of course, would have the end result of controlling others' behaviors."

Fitzhugh gave a start, disturbing the somnolent Lily, who uttered a mewl of protest. But I could tell that his reaction was not due to the information being unfamiliar; rather, he was amazed that anyone else might have knowledge of it.

"You have heard of this, haven't you?" Juno remarked in her quietly assertive way.

In response, Fitzhugh rose, after having gently displaced Lily, who resumed her coiled position in the warmth of the now vacant chair. His tall, thin frame was still erect, despite his age, with only a slight curving of his shoulders. Making his way with surprising rapidity, he disappeared into the maze of stacks. We were left to stare at each other in curiosity; his rude departure did not offend, as his eccentricities were legendary. Kipp seemed to take all things in stride and in his sponge-like manner soaked up the atmosphere.

Fitzhugh soon returned, carrying a large binder. Choosing to not disturb Lily, he pulled another chair close to his desk where he rested the series of ancient manuscripts. The expression on his face was best described as furtive.

"What I am about to share can never leave this room."

We glanced at one another, knowing we were all obviously navigating a bog of uncertainty these days, just trying to avoid the quicksand that lay somnolent and malignant beneath our feet. Telepaths, by nature, were not secretive with one another since it required a constant expenditure of energy.

Fitzhugh, after adjusting his reading glasses on his hooked nose, cleared his throat and began to read:

The following story was told by Sir William of York to Elledge in the year 1543:

I fancied myself a traveler who specialized in military history. In many ways, I followed the lead of my father, who was rather renowned for his exploits. I spent many of my years studying the military methods of the ancient Romans; my father, Ranwulf, along with his symbiont, Datis, always seemed to prefer the East. My father told me, in shattering detail, of the demise of King Leonidas I at Thermopylae. The Persians finally, with superior numbers and the assistance of a traitor, wore him down.

But I digress, since my purpose here today is to tell you of my adventures with the Roman Army under Julius Caesar during the wars in what was referred to as Germannica. Having spent many years working my way upwards in the ranks, I had become an aide de camp to one of Caesar's generals and was considered to be a valued confidant. My symbiont, Renny, was to all appearances my loyal dog and was (to his amusement) the divisional pet.

We had made camp in the lower Rhine valley when a very curious event occurred. What appeared to be a canine appeared on the outskirts of our encampment; he was a large, wolf-like creature, and the camp dogs immediately took off in pursuit. He evaded them with ease, but every evening he would appear thus, dancing on the edge of our firelights, only then to evaporate zephyr-like into the fog and mists. After days of this, the men became somewhat uneasy; there was an unearthly quality about the creature. The more superstitious among them had branded our canine visitor a wraith.

One night, I was walking towards the edge of camp to take care of my needs, accompanied as always by my beloved Renny. I had just escaped the last fading circle of light when the mysterious dog appeared, no greater than 20 steps away from me. Renny bared his teeth and growled, but just as suddenly stopped as he recognized (as did I in that moment) that what appeared to be a dog was in actuality a lupine *symbiont*. His mind was singularly powerful and his projected thoughts poured into our minds so that we knew his essence in but a moment of time.

"I am Eli," he said, in introduction.

Renny and I checked to see that we were unobserved and then we left the last tiny fragments of fire light behind in order to join our new companion. The three of us walked to a small glen, led by the dappled glow of the partial moon. After we settled ourselves, Eli commenced to share his history. He was an aged *symbiont,* estimating that he had seen at least 923 winters; the shadow of death was upon him, as he waited here, alone, in these forested hills. As my eyes examined him, I noted his grizzled muzzle and the stiffness of his gait on legs that were plagued by rheumatism. His eyes, opaquely clouded, met mine; indeed, Eli appeared to be blind in one eye and the vision in the remaining eye was swiftly being lost. Soon Eli would be totally blind, unable to fend for himself. His destiny was set, but all I could sense from him was a welcomed peace. There was a lifetime of pain in this one, I thought, curious to learn his story.

"If you won't find me ill mannered," Eli began, as he tucked his legs under his thin body and lay carefully on the carpet of leaves, "it will serve me well if I can rest as we talk."

"May we bring you food so that you might sup?" I began, worried for his well being, but he halted me by politely declining my offer.

"No, with gratitude, but I need to tell of my history before my time is gone. I have searched for years, looking for a *symbiont* with whom I can share, and it would seem that destiny has proclaimed it will be you and Renny." He glanced at Renny who briefly wagged his tail before laying down close by the elderly Eli. I read enough of Renny's mind to know he was hoping he could share his body warmth with the ancient one as the chill of nighttime began to close in about us. Eli took a breath and continued his story.

"I am the last in the line of lupine *symbionts* who were different from all others. Due to that difference, we have been hounded from the community of *symbionts* and left, without the balancing half of the humanoid, to survive on our own. The hope being, of course, that we would eventually die off."

I was horrified; as a *symbiont,* the cruelest event that could overtake us would be to not be allowed the joining that made us complete. And why would a group of *symbionts* want any family or group to die off with no progeny? What was Eli's secret?

Eli raised his head for moment, and I saw the shadow of his former self, when he had been strong and powerful—a noble creature. He had pride but recognized the reaction in me as being a shade of pity and realized I had a kind heart towards him.

"In ancient times, there was a branch of the lupine family that developed some different, enhanced skills from the other lupines or humanoids. These *symbionts* had the usual abilities that were universally shared but in addition could plant thoughts in the minds of other beings, thus guiding and controlling their behaviors." He stopped for a moment, so that Renny and I could digest what had been said. Continuing, he added, "And I am the last of that line, the last of my kind. When I die, that difference will die with me."

I sputtered, not sure what to say. "But Eli, how could this be? I have never heard of this."

"Secrets are difficult to keep concealed, but the stories in regards to me and my kind have died off over the ages. To be sure, myths abounded, but I will be the last alive to share the story with any veracity. When the early humanoids and other lupines realized there were those in their midst who had the potential to make them dance like puppets, they became both alarmed and envious of these lupines that were specially gifted. There were efforts made to suppress any further breeding of the males, who seemed to pass along this ability; all of the afflicted lupines were not allowed a symbiotic bond." He paused for a moment before adding, "They were not able to trust us."

"How did you manage to hide yourself away?" Renny asked.

"It would seem that whatever made us different has taken generations to die out. If any lupine mother recognized that her young pup had what had been labeled a cursed ability, she was forced to either leave the group and fend for herself and her child or hide the fact as best she could. My mother chose to take me and leave. She told me that I was gifted and to never be ashamed." He paused and his feelings for his mother, who had loved him so intensely that she would leave her community and family, threatened to overwhelm him.

"My mother was proud of me," he added with a catch in his thoughts.

Renny inched closer and gently placed his soft muzzle along the narrow flank of Eli, a gesture of comfort and acceptance. Eli inwardly smiled.

"It has been a long time since I have felt the touch of another. Thank you, my brother."

He continued with his story. "I have spent countless years, wandering, looking for other *symbionts*. In my early days, whenever I would approach others, they would mark me for what I was and hound me from their midst. It was as if I, an innocent, was branded with the mark of the evil beast." He paused and slightly shifted his position.

"Forgive me; if I stay too long in one place, I become stiff and it is difficult to rise."

"Please, Eli," I began, "I beg you; let me bring you sustenance, perhaps a warm blanket, anything to make you more comfortable."

He again politely demurred and continued his narrative.

"I finally ceased my wanderings in search of like beings. Instead, I would stay close to villages, encampments—anywhere human beings were gathered—and I would share vicariously in their lives. I could, of course, read their thoughts and took part in their happiness, their despair, and this gave me some measure of community."

There was I, an adult humanoid *symbiont*, having seen countless battles with men dying, maimed in war, and I felt the warmth of tears spill unbidden from my eyes and down my weathered cheeks. Suddenly, the thoughts of Eli were there to reassure me; his life had been good, one of adventure. He wanted us to honor his passing with joyfulness.

"Eli, will you show me this ability of yours, so that I will understand it for the sake of our people and history?" I asked.

"Well, to some degree, I have already done that. Did you not wonder how I so easily evaded the camp dogs who rushed out with my every approach? Surely you have noted, from my appearance, that I am no longer strong or fleet."

As I considered his words, it seemed that time passed in a void and I looked around to find myself some ten strides away from Eli and Renny, the latter of whom was staring at me in fascination. I was struggling to reconcile what was odd about the moment, and then I realized I was standing erect, balanced on my right foot, while I held my left leg high in the air with my foot extended. It occurred to me that I was thinking I needed to be doing just that, standing in that silly manner. Slowly, I lowered my foot, with the realization that Eli had done what I asked.

I walked back to where my lupine friends were waiting and sank slowly to the ground. All of this was difficult to sort out. Eli was looking at me, his clouded eyes suddenly bright in the dimly lit forest. The three of us sat quietly for a time, the solitude only broken with sounds from the now distant Roman encampment as well as the gentle hum of the woods. Eli's mind reached out to us like a caress.

"I need to leave you now," he began, interrupting me when I tried to cut him off. "No, my brother, I have done what I set out to do, and now I must go. My time is near, and I have prepared the place for my final rest."

Renny tried to convince him to let us accompany him so that his last moments would not be in solitude, but he refused.

"I have spent the majority of my life in isolation; it would be unnatural for me to have companions in death. Do not worry my friends; the solitary way is familiar to me, and I have no fear. You have done immeasurable good today in allowing me to finish my circle of life by telling my story." He paused for a moment before adding, "I can rest now."

He slowly rose, and, without a backward glance, he disappeared into the darkness. That was the first and last time we saw Eli; nor did we feel his presence in subsequent days. Renny and I, with heavy hearts, returned to camp and resumed our charade. Until the end of my days, I will be haunted by the story of Eli.

Fitzhugh paused, resting his aged hands reverently on the manuscript before closing the binder and centering it carefully on the oak desk.

Philo asked, "So you knew of this sort of thing?"

Fitzhugh appeared to be considering his words carefully before giving a measured reply.

"There is an entire section of manuscripts filled with the unexplainable. I have not made it a habit to share those stories with others."

"Why not?" Juno asked.

"There have been, in the distant past, efforts made to suppress certain information. Indeed, at one point I had to secret certain manuscripts away, lest the mob destroy them in their self righteous zeal to modify our history."

Philo said, "That sounds like something humans do—

and on a routine basis—but I am disappointed that we *symbionts* would be capable of the same behavior."

I was sitting quietly (something unusual for me), Kipp by my side; I gently reached out with my mind to see how he was dealing with these new revelations. Our eyes met and the warmth of his amber gaze reassured me; Kipp was without a doubt the most balanced creature I had ever met. He knew exactly who he was, despite the rest of us being a little confused right now. I think we were struggling with old demons, a burden Kipp did not share.

CHAPTER 11

We retired home, following our evening with Fitzhugh. Sleep came with difficulty and I awoke the next morning feeling as if I had fought dragons all night. A hesitant glance in the mirror over my wash basin revealed a face that was pale and etched with lines of exhaustion. Kipp had, at my instruction, ceased his dream manipulations. I reassured him that it was natural and acceptable for beings to struggle with unpleasantness; indeed, it strengthened us if we allowed it to do so.

We faced another rigorous day at Technicorps, so I prepared myself by ingesting large amounts of strong coffee. Our little trio had quickly settled into a comfortable routine of beginning our day together in the garden during the early morning hours. With my mug of brew in hand, I would watch with fascination as Kipp and Lily explored their natural world.

Kipp, as Lily's surrogate mother, had taken on the role of her tutor. He patiently showed her how to prowl, pounce, and play, as well as generally relate to nature. It would be odd, as Lily grew, to see her acting more like a dog than a cat. I will give Kipp credit, however—he did attempt to demonstrate typical feline predatory creeping by getting down on his stomach, haunches jacked up behind him in an awkward stance. It really was quite amusing. At one point, Lily tired of instruction and attacked Kipp's right foreleg, encircling it with her legs, kicking, biting and scratching. He tried to dislodge her but couldn't; he finally limped to me and I managed to pull her free.

"That isn't funny," Kipp declared, in response to my unspoken thoughts.

But it was.

I readied myself for the day with my customary ritual of minimal preparations. It wasn't exactly that I didn't care about my appearance; it is just that after several hundred years, there are only so many variations on the same palette. Kipp always watched me with curiosity, fascinated by the extra steps needed for me to prepare to face the public versus his, which consisted of a good shake, licking a forepaw and a big yawn. He really didn't know how little I did in contrast to many others. I think I still had a nice dress somewhere but was unable to locate it. And if I had found it, I did not possess appropriate shoes. On the floor of my closet, there was a pair of hiking boots, some running shoes and a pair of ancient flip flops. Standing there, hands on hips, one thing was clear to me: I didn't have to struggle between choices, that much was certain. I guess in some circles that might qualify as part of a stress reduction lifestyle. Finally I remembered that my jeans were in the dryer along with a pullover. Retrieving them, I finished dressing and, after running a brush through my tangled hair and clipping it back from my face, we left for the day.

The weather was flawless, so we walked, enjoying the bracing edge of coolness. I had procured a little carrier for Lily that resembled a front body infant carrier. So she was strapped to me for a change, giving Kipp's jaws a rest. As we traversed the two miles to Technicorps, I told Kipp of a place that I'd found in the midst of Duke Forest.

"Kipp, as many times as I've walked by and explored

it, I can't explain it. In the dark of the woods there is a copse—a thicket of trees—and I swear, it glows with a pale light. I even showed it to Philo once and he was mystified, too. True, there are breaks in the canopy that allow sunlight to hit the forest floor, but the illumination in this place just looks different, odd." I promised him we would go there as soon as we could get free from our current obligations.

We arrived a little early, so we dropped down to see Fitzhugh at Kipp's bequest. Usually the chronicler was unhappy to have visitors, but his face actually lit up upon seeing Kipp and Lily. He was never excited to see me. After a brief chat, he offered to keep Lily with him for the day while we went about our business. We made our way to the large conference room and were ushered in with alacrity. Obviously, the Twelve had been waiting for us, even though my watch showed we were on time. Well, I thought, just another black mark on my already sullied record. Philo rose and greeted us.

"Petra, Kipp, please be seated." He motioned to a vacant chair and bench. As we walked by Juno, she and Kipp briefly touched noses in greeting. I was aware that both Philo and Juno were carefully guarding their new knowledge about Kipp.

"We've been discussing all the issues," he continued, "and would like to do the following, if it's acceptable to you both."

He paused and slowly walked around the room, but I knew him well enough to recognize his restless energy for what it was. Glancing at Max Stone, I picked up on his curiosity; he thought something was underneath all the polite exchange, but he didn't know what.

"Petra," Philo said, "we would like for you to conduct some research in anticipation of an investigative journey." Before I could say anything, he added, "But slowly, and on your own time. We recognize your body is still in recovery mode from your last trip, and we're in no hurry for you to undertake the next one."

"And Kipp?" I asked.

Juno spoke at that point.

"I want Kipp to spend time with me for a while, exclusively, with no more interrogations by the twelve of us."

I felt a stab of anxiety in Kipp.

"What do you mean, Juno, by 'exclusively'?" I asked, keeping my voice neutral with effort.

Max stood up, predictably agitated with me.

"I knew we could expect this type of overbearing behavior from you. You are not in charge here; your job is to do what we tell you to do, and with as few comments and editorials as possible." He stopped himself with effort, his face red.

I couldn't help myself and retorted, "Why don't you read my thoughts right now, Max, since I have some good advice for you about what you can do with yourself."

"Okay, okay, everyone calm down," Philo said, walking over to clap Max on the shoulder. "We are here to help Kipp assimilate; also it's our job to help Petra prepare for her next assignment." He paused and glanced at me. "And, Petra, that sort of exchange is not helpful at all, so please try to control yourself."

Kipp stood up, suddenly.

"I don't need all of you talking around me or for me, either," he said, with a glance at me. "I will tell you what I'm willing to do." He paused and glanced down the table at the others; in that moment I've never been as proud of another being as I was of him.

"I'd like to spend time with Juno, as I think she can teach me what it means to be a lupine *symbiont*. But I'm bonded to Petra, and my commitment is to her. So I will come here each day and work with Juno, but at the end of the day, I'll go home with Petra. I will not be separated from her, so if any of you are thinking that, you're sadly mistaken."

I could tell this wasn't what they had in mind. But they

could definitely read Kipp's intent and he was solidly planted and would not be budged. And despite Max's outburst, *symbionts* typically avoided overbearing, controlling behavior. It was just not part and parcel of our hardwiring as a species.

"Well, Kipp," Philo said, "we hear you and obviously we cannot force you to do anything against your will, nor would we ever want to. So I think that we can certainly do this as you've suggested."

We were told that we could take the rest of the day off. After retrieving Lily, we decided to go to Duke Forest so that Kipp could see my magical grove of trees. The weather was quite pleasant as fall edged closer. With a quick stop by my house, I changed into my hiking togs and off we went, Kipp with his head sticking out the window of my tiny, underused car. After a mild disagreement—which I lost—the ever present Lily was again in our company and underfoot.

We quickly disappeared into the dense woods, and I verged off the main trail onto one that was seldom used by most hikers, it being a bit too rough for casual walking. Kipp eventually broke the silence after about 45 minutes of brisk walking.

"I hope we don't have to go into that conference room again." He paused before adding, "It always seems to end in some sort of unpleasant argument."

"Kipp, I apologize. I lost my temper with Max. It was, well, unseemly."

He looked at me, and I could read his amusement.

"No, you're not sorry, and it doesn't matter anyway. I don't like him either. You were torn between wanting to slap him or yawn in his face."

As had become accepted between us, Kipp had access to all parts of my mind. He would learn control so that other *symbionts* would not feel violated by his impressive telepathic range. But I was not threatened by him and wanted his relationship to me to be as natural as possible. It was only in the evolution of our species that we had learned to be repressive. He darted off for a minute to chase after Lily, who had scooted between some dense foliage. They both disappeared from my view for a few moments.

About twenty feet away, to the left of the trail, was my glowing copse of trees. Kipp and Lily bounded back into view and he stopped, following the direction of my gaze. We approached and I took note of the trees in the vicinity: black cherry, sweet birch, hackberry and white ash. My little thicket glowed with a blue white illumination; in contrast, elsewhere the light obtained by filtered sun rays was amber-yellow in hue. Kipp was as fascinated as was I; even though he lacked my color discrimination abilities, he could tell that the lighting was unusual. Lily had no opinion, of course. This was one moment when her primitive simplicity had a negative aspect: she could not appreciate the beauty displayed before us.

Ahead was the remnant of an ancient oak, one that had fallen years before but was too stubborn to have rotted away yet. It was there we took our rest. It didn't require much telepathy on my part to discern that Kipp had obviously been holding on to his curiosity, waiting for the right moment to pose his query.

"Petra, you know that I trust you completely. Why would Philo and Juno have gone along with the others in wanting to separate us, even if temporarily?"

"I don't have an answer for that, but I still trust them. They may have wanted the rest of the group to think they are in control of you, and they did that by entrusting you to Juno." I paused for a moment as I considered my thoughts on the matter.

"But in any case, Juno will be a good mentor for you, much better than am I." I put my arm around his massive neck and pulled him close. "And that's not false modesty, my dear one, just the truth."

That solitary moment in the forest was to be our last for a long while. Our business at Technicorps became all consuming for the next several weeks. Kipp started his days early with Juno and stayed with her until evening. I, on the other hand, was given an assignment by Philo, the first task of which was to build my strength back in anticipation of a time journey. Second, I would meet with Fitzhugh, who would prepare me with historical records for analysis and review. Philo and I went together so that he could make the appropriate requests from the irritable Fitzhugh. Down we went to the lowest level, and found the recluse in his lair. The young apprentice, Peter, met us and at Fitzhugh's command was sent to prepare a pot of hot tea, his one vice and the only thing he was ever willing to share. Philo, after gently dislodging Lily from his targeted chair, took his seat. The rambunctious Lily was spending her days with the doting Fitzhugh and Peter while Kipp and I were occupied elsewhere.

"Fitzhugh," Philo began, "the Twelve have an assignment for Petra and Kipp, and we need you to help her prepare by pulling your archives of the Lost Colony at Roanoke Island."

Fitzhugh's eyebrows shot up and he commented, "Nicholas Elliott made that journey in 1965, and it is all well chronicled what happened to the settlers of the colony in 1587. What on earth could Petra investigate there that has not already been done?"

Philo smiled thinly.

"It is not the exploration of the Lost Colony of 1587 that is in question. I recall, however, that Elliott mentioned that there was another colony, one sandwiched in between the initial one established in 1585, and the second one of 1587. It would be an investigation of an event in time that has gone unrecorded in history, just the sort of thing that's right up Petra's, well, uh, alley."

Fitzhugh took a moment to stare at me and did not bother to guard his thoughts which were not complementary of me, my skills or anyone's assumption of what my alley might be.

"Peter, go and fetch the manuscripts. No, wait, I will go and do it myself, and you can follow and watch and learn something for a change."

Peter raised his eyebrows at us but followed meekly. The life of an apprentice was fraught with unpleasantness, I mused, feeling some compassion for the lad. Fitzhugh soon returned with a massive manual and, after studying it for a few moments, opened it to the aforementioned section.

"Here, help yourself. Take it to the table over there and make yourself at home. Peter and I were working, so if you will excuse us, please...."

Philo hefted the book with effort and carried it to the desk for me.

"Petra, I will leave you to it. I want you to read all of Elliot's work and concentrate especially on the final chapter."

I sat for a moment enjoying the atmosphere of the library, the cluttered nature of which reminded me of my home. A musty odor, the result of hundreds of years of parchment and paper compressed in a relatively small area, surrounded me like a fog. Fitzhugh received his nourishment from these dim, claustrophobic catacombs; it was like mother's milk to him. The furniture, as it were, was mostly rogue pieces, probably hand-me-downs found at antique stores and second hand shops. I chose a chair, one designed to keep me awake with its puritan upright back and woven cane seat. Glancing around, I appreciated anew Fitzhugh's choice of color— he avoided the typical industrial putty color that seemed the hallmark of most office buildings. Instead, he had used the deep, rich green of the Victorian era, a shade seen in so many country estates. Peter arrived at that moment with the hot tea.

"So, Miss Goodgame, they are going to send you on another journey?" he asked, his eyes wide with curiosity.

"So it seems, Peter." I took a sip of the very hot tea,

burning my upper lip in the process.

"I wish I could do something like that rather than being stuck here all day with Fitzhugh." He glanced quickly over his shoulder, but Fitzhugh was not in sight.

"You remember, don't you, that he can read your mind, Peter? So talking quietly really doesn't help."

Peter rolled his eyes.

"Oh, he knows already how I feel about it. My mother didn't want me to travel; she thinks it is too dangerous. I don't even have a *symbiont*, yet."

I smiled, acknowledging how difficult it is to be young in the midst of so much excitement.

"Peter, there are many downsides to traveling. And remember this—those of us who travel are completely dependent on Fitzhugh's historical records to assist us in our assignments. So what you are doing down here is critically important, even if it doesn't feel that way right now." I knew that didn't sooth his angst, but it was true.

We both heard Fitzhugh call for him and, with a sigh, he hurried off. My tea had cooled to a tolerable temperature, so I settled myself to read the volumes of notes before me.

CHAPTER 12

Nicholas Elliott's manuscript of his investigation of the Lost Colony was extensive, since he began his journey in England in order to assume the identity of one of the future colonists. Subsequently he made the lengthy sea voyage to the New World, landed, and participated in the creation of the colony. It must have been difficult to be involved and work with them, without interfering in the natural evolution towards their destiny. Of course, this was always the challenge laid at the feet of the researcher. I had never personally met Elliott, but he was legendary as a disciplined and talented *symbiont*—as was his companion, Sancia.

Over a period of six weeks, I plowed through the volumes, reading some 650 pages of eye-popping detail. In preparation for my upcoming assignment, I interspersed my study with physical exercise and strengthening. Technicorps had an onsite gymnasium which, to the humans who worked at the company, was framed to be a fabulous employer benefit. In actuality, it served a functional purpose for the traveling *symbionts*— we needed a place to physically prepare for the rigors of travel and the associated deprivation and hardship. Pushing the manuscripts aside, I made my way to the fitness center where I had an appointment with Kyle.

The sole *symbiont* who worked there, he was surrounded by human trainers and assistants who were ignorant of his true identity.

"Hello, Petra," he said, smiling as I walked up. "I haven't seen you in a long time."

"Hi, Kyle" I responded. "Yes, it's been a while. I just recently returned from a journey and the Twelve have already got me scheduled to go out again soon. So I need some help, please."

The smile faded from his face.

"I heard about Tula and I'm truly sorry. She was highly regarded by all of us."

Tactfully, he moved on and together we worked out a daily program of endurance and strengthening exercises. He also reviewed and recommended nutritional needs, which were different than for humans. I was not unfamiliar with most of this information, since I was no novice and made a mental note to do better. Perhaps less coffee and ice cream and more healthy protein would be the right move to make if I could manage to exert a little more discipline.

I'd made my way to the weight set and was about to begin some arm and chest exercises, when Jeff, a human who worked in the research division, approached. He had expressed his interest in me previously, but I consistently rebuffed him—politely but firmly. Relationships between humans and *symbionts* were not forbidden but were always unwise. I made it a personal policy to nip such things in the bud—and quickly.

"Petra, you're back!" he exclaimed, having been told that I was out of town on a sabbatical. Before I could stop him, he reached out and gave me a full body hug.

"I missed seeing you here." Not missing a beat and without giving me time to respond, he added, "How about grabbing something to eat with me later?"

Jeff was a very nice man, and I could divine his earnest intent, but I also knew he was too attracted to me and that there would be no way I could keep our relationship at a friendship level. And what kind of friend could I possibly be if I had to basically lie about who I was? His open face and clear eyes added to an overall appearance of vulnerability. What could I say to deter him, kindly, but for good?

"Jeff, I'm involved with someone new, and I don't think it would be appropriate for me to go out with you under the circumstances." As did all *symbionts*, I possessed the ability to lie with ease, but this was only a partial lie; I was newly associated with Kipp, as it were.

His face fell in disappointment, but he didn't push me any further. He did add, as he turned away, "Well, he is a lucky man, and I wish you well."

Kyle walked up to tease me a bit, but, after a glance at my face, he decided discretion to be the better part of valor and instead coached me on a more efficient chest press. After a couple of hours of work, I showered and ran back downstairs to continue with my studies. Nearing the end of Elliott's story, I had not seen any clue about the fabled third colony. Just as I was thinking I had wasted my time, I came upon the following passages:

The following is a postscript to my narrative of the true occurrences that took place at Roanoke Island, from the years 1587 to 1589.

Upon the arrival of the hundred plus settlers who were brought to Roanoke Island by John White in the year 1587, there was general knowledge among all of us that there had been an initial colony established on the island in 1585; there was also another colony established in 1586, on a point slightly inland from the shore on the mainland. (In modern days, this location would be at the northernmost tip of Dare County, North Carolina.)

After our group was deposited abruptly by our Portuguese pilot on the same island of the 1585 settlement, John White, having acquired a small boat (by undisclosed means), directed a company of men to navigate the Roanoke Sound in order to check on the status of the colonists who had been left on the mainland the previous year. I, along with the other Roanoke Island colonists, was never told what happened, but the boat returned, and all aboard her seemed shaken by their visit to the colony. The leader of the group met in conference with White, bringing with him a metal strongbox that seemed securely locked to our eyes. Afterwards, a distressed John White emerged, and, refusing to give any details, he told those of us congregated that no one was left alive on the mainland.

When John White left us to return to England, he apparently took the strongbox with him, and there was never any more public discussion of the event. Indeed, when anyone tried to question any of the men who had visited the Land's Point colony—as it had come to be named—he would be met with disapprobation.

I am at the end of my days of traveling, at least to such primitive locals. The years of trips, during which my body suffers so much physical and mental stress, have taken their toll. I will leave this narrative in the hopes that perhaps one day someone will chose to visit the aforementioned locale and ascertain the fate of the colonists of Land's Point.

I sat back, intrigued. And, I might add, curious that the Twelve would identify this time journey as being of importance, in the context of there being such little evidence that the Land's Point colony had even existed. For all we knew, John White had planted a seed of fear purposely, perhaps to keep the Roanoke Island settlers from journeying to the mainland. After asking permission to use the computer, I pulled up some topographical maps of the area and studied the North Carolina coastline with interest. I would ask Philo for permission to take Kipp on a little road trip so that we could get a sense of the lay of the land. Experience had taught me that when one has very little information to use for planning a time journey, it can be of help to physically visit the locale. I don't know why, but it does enhance the process; maybe *symbionts* have some type of genetic ability to divine the past from a location.

Calling Peter to assist me, we chased Lily all over the library so that I could gather her up to go home. She was in a particularly frisky mood and actually climbed one of the shelves as if it were a tree. Peter dragged over a ladder and managed to peel her off of the top shelf where she clung to a leather binder. Way too much work from my way of thinking. Kipp met me outside and was excited to share his day with Juno. Using my mind, I could see how her influence was helping him to be even more balanced and confident, if that was possible. She was apparently concentrating on ethics and our code of noninterference, as well as trying to help him learn how to use his enhanced skills in an appropriate manner. I, in turn, shared, and told Kipp of what I'd learned about the Land's Point colony and the upcoming drive to the coast for environmental immersion. No one loved a ride in the car more than Kipp, so his tail wagged furiously at my disclosure.

After having discussed my plan with Philo, who gave his blessings, we started out to Dare County, leaving the rambunctious Lily in the care of Fitzhugh, who was delighted to have been chosen to be her godfather. Who would have known he was capable of such affection? It was a beautiful day and the sky looming over us was a spectacularly vivid color of intense blue, totally free of clouds. To amuse Kipp, the car windows were lowered and we literally breezed our way along Highway 64, which ran from Durham to Mann's Harbor. From there, we snaked our way north, driving as far as we could conceivably go, trying to find the uppermost point of land. Of course, it was different now from the time of Land's Point Colony, since progress and habitation had changed the landscape. After a while, I pulled the car over at the edge of a small park. We were probably about a half of a mile inland from the Roanoke Sound. I could easily smell the ocean and feel the breeze unique to the Atlantic. Kipp joined me, and we found a small grassy area beneath a large oak.

"Okay, Kipp, begin to imagine it. The year is 1586; somewhere close by, a small colony of men and perhaps women have hacked a fortress out of the forest. Think about the land—the primordial forest would have been dense, thinning as it approached the shoreline nearby. There would have been a large number of downed trees, the victims of countless ages of hurricanes and severe ocean storms. The large trees would lie rotting on the ground; stubborn, they're reluctant to give up their grasp of the earth.

"The forest would have been teeming with life. Native Americans, ancient to the land, viewed the newcomers with anxiety; they didn't know it yet, but their civilization would one day be compromised by these interlopers. Deer, bear, wolves, panthers, all made up some of the larger animals, predators and prey engaged in their ancient contest for survival." I sounded a little dramatic but was enjoying the moment, feeling like a storyteller.

"Close your eyes, Kipp, and concentrate on this place. Try and think of it transformed into its natural state."

Kipp did as I bade him. I could feel him begin to relax and concentrate. His breathing slowed down, becoming deep and regular. This was interesting to me, as he could immediately and on command place himself in this meditative state. I didn't know if he just could do this naturally or if Juno had been teaching him. Either way, it was an impressive display of self control, and it put my own meager abilities to shame. I reached down and dug my fingers into the soil, bringing up the fistful of dark earth to my face. Inhaling deeply, I mentally tried to connect myself with the history of the place, letting my mind wander throughout the imagined past. Ordinarily, I might have prepared for a journey with simple research, but the paucity of information available about the Land's Point colony had forced me to be more creative. We would be entering into a void in the past with no beginning and no end.

Looking down, I saw that Kipp had actually stretched out on his side and appeared to be sleeping. But his mind remained alert and active, just intensely focused. I lay down next to him and together we reclined on the grass beneath the oak, the bright sun shaded, its dappled light falling over us in a chaotic pattern. With a little effort, I marshaled control over my thoughts and began to match Kipp's breathing so that we were gradually becoming synchronized. This was good practice, for our ability to do this, and do it well, was necessary for our time journeys. I felt Kipp lazily and effortlessly merge his thoughts with mine and he unconsciously thumped his tail on the ground in pleasure. His love and attachment surrounded us like the air we breathed.

"I love you, too," I said, audibly.

After a few hours, we returned to our motel room with a takeout dinner of grilled chicken for Kipp and a sandwich for me. He found a new delight in a food that was not healthy for either of us: French fries. Together, we wolfed down a large portion, most of them drenched in ketchup.

"I've pretty much figured out the work part of what *symbionts* do, but what do you do when you aren't traveling in time on a particular job? How do you have fun? And how do you blend your lives with that of humans?" Kipp launched this rapid fire trio of questions as I selected a particularly enticing looking French fry to consume.

"Well, all traveling *symbionts* are allowed to take a trip for their own interest—just for fun—once in a blue moon as a bonus of sort. It usually is something that is low risk and effortless."

"So, what sort of bonus trip have you taken?" Kipp was licking a stain of ketchup from his forepaw.

"Well, for example, I travelled back so that I could watch some of the work to create the sculptures of the

four presidents on Mount Rushmore. That's a good
example of a fun trip with no particular mystery
attached. But on the other hand, my, uh, secular job, if
you want to call it that, is a historian who specializes in
the American Civil War, and I have made numerous
trips back to witness history. I find, when I lecture to
students, that my first hand knowledge gives me a
passion that makes the discussion a bit more interesting
than the usual dry material."

"So, do you meet people or witness events?" he asked.

"Both," I replied. "I saw countless men die on the
battlefield and witnessed amazing acts of courage. War
was literally hell and combat was frequently hand to
hand; the weapons inflicted terrible damage due to the
type of armaments used."

"Did you meet anyone of note?"

"Well, over the years I have made many visits to that
span of time and was fortunate to meet Robert E. Lee as
well as U.S. Grant. I grieved with the Yankees over the
death of General McPherson, who was greatly loved,
and shed tears with the butternuts when Stonewall
Jackson died."

"I don't understand how any of that can be fun," Kipp
commented.

"That was not fun—just part of my job. It was
exciting, sad, tragic and motivational—all at once. I, one
day, need to go back so I can do some work around the
siege of Atlanta. I never met Sherman and understand he
was an unusual character. He was brilliant, aggressive
and of a very excitable nature. Early on, he was not a
major player due to what others considered to be mental
instability. But Grant trusted him implicitly. The defense
of Atlanta was suddenly left to an untested General
Hood—from a historian's perspective, it is all
fascinating."

"Can I go with you?" he asked, before realizing how silly
that sounded. In order for me to travel, he had to go as my
partner. I simply rolled my eyes at him in response.

"Actually, Philo was hinting that I might be in store for a bonus fun trip soon. I think after the previous one and this upcoming assignment, I'll need something that is a little less intense."

"What would it be? Where would we go?" he asked.

"I have no idea. We would have to sit down together and work it out."

We glanced at the remaining French fries and both, politely, waited for the other to decline.

"It is my hope that when I lecture students about the war, they will gain some understanding of how critical a thorough knowledge of history can be. I don't varnish it, politicize it or try to make it comfortable. The sacrifices of all should be honored, and I intend to make certain the truth is not lost in time."

I decided to take Kipp on a loop on our return trip home so that he could see the Atlantic Ocean. So after a good night of restful sleep, we awoke early and crossed over the Croatan Sound, picking up Highway 12, proceeding southward along the Outer Banks. Kipp was mesmerized and kept his big head stuck out of the ocean facing window. His nostrils were busy as he canvassed the area, no doubt able to pick up the myriad of life forms associated with the sea. We stopped at Avon and ran down to the sandy shore. Kipp darted along the edge of the water, letting the lapping waves overtake his quick feet. The Atlantic lacked the turquoise color of the Gulf—the steely gray color was endless. Somehow to me it had always seemed more ominous.

"Petra, so people sailed on vessels made of wood across this water to come to America?"

"Yes. So try to envision a storm, the waves forty feet high, as people and goods packed on wooden ships were tossed about. They had to be sturdy stock and brave to come to such an unknown and potentially hostile place."

Kipp was quiet, absorbing the beauty of the place. Even in this age, there would always be a wild, untamed nature to the sea. I filled my mind with pictures of whales, fish, rays, sharks and anything else I could think of, even the diminutive seahorse. Kipp, borrowing the creations of my mind, was fascinated that these mysterious depths could conceal so much. After walking silently along the shore, we made our way back to the car and continued south to Ocracoke Island; there, we picked up the ferry to the mainland. It was late that evening before we arrived home. After a quick meal, we fell into bed. Morning would come too soon.

We made our usual walk to the office the next day, and, after dropping by Fitzhugh's office to visit with Lily and thank him for having tended to her, Kipp returned to his work with Juno while I visited the preparations laboratory. There, *symbionts* who specialized in garments, currencies, period customs, etc. were ready to assist me in preparing for the rudiments I would need in order to form a believable character. In medieval times, I suppose this would have been the role of the armorer and his ilk. After some discussion, I gave them the project as envisioned. Of course, everything depended on the approval of the Twelve.

I asked for a time to present my proposal for approval, and Philo informed me that the Twelve would make room for me the next day. Sooner than I thought, but I felt ready. After the hoped-for approval, I could continue with preparations for a few more weeks. That night, as Kipp and I settled in for the evening, I told him of my ideas and he was in concurrence. He had been so consumed with Juno that there had been little time for mutual planning. Kipp nestled close to me; Lily was sandwiched somewhere in between us. There was one pitiful meow of protest as she was squashed in the midst of a *symbiont* sandwich, and then we all fell asleep, exhausted.

The day came too soon, and I dressed with more care than usual, hoping my attention to detail would impress the Twelve. As Kipp and I were ushered into the inner sanctum, I casually canvassed the room for superficial impressions. There appeared to be a fairly even flow of emotions—only minor ripples—and certainly no strong negatives to my brief assessment.

Philo took the lead.

"Petra, Kipp, so glad you are both here. Please be seated." After a moment he asked, "Can we offer you anything?" We both responded in the negative.

"Okay, Petra, you're on; tell us what you have."

I stood, feeling more awkward than usual. Kipp's reassuring mind reached out to touch mine, a mental hand-hold of sorts.

"After study and careful reflection, I've decided to assume the role of a widow in her late twenties, who is the offspring of a Spanish father and an English mother. I took to the seas with my father, the Spaniard, following the death of my husband. My father was a trader who terminated his allegiance to Spain in deference of my mother. He chose a neutral path and sailed to various exotic ports as well as some of the New World colonies, both English as well as Spanish. My plan was to appear at the colony and tell them that my father's ship foundered, and that I was the sole survivor. I would appear of middle class, with some education but more experience from travel with my father. To the colonists, I would look exotic, hoping that any suspicions that would be generated by my sudden appearance with Kipp would be negated, or at least diminished by the vulnerability of a woman alone in the wilderness." I paused for a minute to gather my thoughts and was interrupted by Juno who asked how Kipp would be explained.

"Uh, I had planned to tell them that he was a Chinese red crested mastiff."

Philo smiled and Kipp laughed, enjoying being the target of my creative imagination.

Without skipping a beat, I continued, "Because, you see, my father sailed to China to trade in exotic fabrics and while there was presented with a puppy which he gave to me, to help my broken heart after my husband died." I paused, glancing around the room in satisfaction.

Max slightly rolled his eyes, but this, as I was doing it, was how it was done. One had to create a role—just like an actor—and play it to the hilt. To fail at this was life threatening. Max, concrete soul that he was, simply could not appreciate unleashed imagination.

Philo suddenly became serious.

"Petra, this is a dangerous journey, since so little is known of this Land's Point colony. To be frank, if it'd been you and Tula, we wouldn't have approved the job."

My eyes met his and I felt unexpected tears threaten to spill.

"But we have so much faith in Kipp and his extraordinary talents, that we think he can make certain the two of you return safely."

The quiet in the room was complete. Not only were there no audible sounds, but also all the minds congregated were utterly still. I stood there, not quite certain how I should respond. Kipp left his bench and quietly padded to my side. He sat, his shoulder pressing into my leg, both comforting me and presenting a literally united presence in the room. My hand drifted down to rest on his broad head.

Kipp shared his assertive thoughts with the others.

"I think we will be ready in two more weeks."

Philo glanced around the room, and, receiving no negative thoughts or comments, he said, "Well, I think that sounds reasonable. Petra, you and Kipp won't need to meet with all of us again, but I'll meet with you both several times to make certain you have all you need for your preparations."

I breathed a sigh of relief and was glad that was done. Now it was back to work for us both.

CHAPTER 13

Following our meeting with the Twelve, Kipp and I made a trip to the preparations division. Having left them earlier with some rough ideas of what we might need, I could now provide better direction. This was one area at Technicorps that was populated by only *symbionts*, and I usually worked with Suzanne. She met me with a broad smile.

"Congratulations, Petra, I'm excited about your new journey." After a pause she added, "And I've looked forward to meeting Kipp." She omitted any comments about Tula, probably to spare my feelings and also to avoid making Kipp feel unwelcome in any way.

I made the introductions and Suzanne led us to her chaotic work area, where a large drafting table was scattered with papers, patterns, fabric swatches, reference books and other bits and pieces.

"Suzanne," I began, "the short version is that I'll be assuming the character of a woman of mixed English and Spanish heritage; my father is a trader and I've spent many years at sea traveling with him to exotic ports. Our ship wrecks on the coast and I'm the sole survivor along with Kipp."

Suzanne began to pace, a behavior characteristic of her when she was deep in thought. She liked to do her thinking out loud, so she began a dialog wherein she painted a visual picture in our minds.

"Let's see. You're on the ship; it hits a shoal, and begins to sink. Your father is trying to shore up the damaged area so that the ship won't go down. He and many of the men are below deck in the hold, but he shouts up orders that the bosun's mate is to take you and disembark on the small boat used for such." She paused for a moment and took a sip of her rapidly cooling coffee. I knew from experience that it was always best to let her finish her train of thought and then inject my own opinions.

"You start to argue, but your father gives you no option. The mate rushes you to your cabin where you grab a few clothing items and shove them in a cotton sack. You make certain to include pieces of your mother's jewelry, a blanket and a water bladder. With those hasty preparations, you dash to the boat and you, Kipp, and the mate are lowered; his instructions were to keep you safe on shore until the ship could be repaired." She paused again, and then asked, "I'm going to make some fresh coffee. Want some?"

"Yes, Suzanne, that would be good for me. Kipp, do you need anything?"

He replied in the negative and settled himself on a pile of fabrics that had fallen to the floor. It was apparent that he was fascinated with the thought processes flowing through the mind of this extremely creative humanoid *symbiont*.

Suzanne reappeared after a few minutes and, after handing me my steaming mug, continued with her rapid stream of ideas.

"I'm thinking of how you might be costumed. You will be going to a colony populated with English settlers— very conservative people, probably middle to upper middle class. We don't know yet if the settlers will be all male or if there will be women there, too. Right?" she added, looking at me.

I nodded my head in the affirmative. "We know the first Roanoke colony was populated by men; the third one was mixed with men and women. This middle settlement is a complete mystery."

Suzanne, charged from the caffeine, was on a roll.

"In the brief you left me, you indicated your character's father traded in fabrics and was widely traveled. So I would see your costume as a little exotic, in comparison to the settlers, but nothing that would make them think you are some sort of wild bohemian. We want them to see you as different but not be rejecting of you. Considering the time of year and the fact you are on a ship, we will go with some woven light wool, and I think you'll need that warmth. We will have a blouse, skirt and weskit; maybe the weskit will be of some bright, patterned fabric, your concession to vanity— perhaps silk from the Orient. Since you have been on a ship, I think we'll go for a real hat—more of a man's hat with a wide brim for shading your face and eyes. I'll have to get our boot maker to start on your shoes. And we'll go into our vault to look at some period jewelry and get to work with reproductions that look the part. It would make sense to think you have a little purse that hangs from a belt with some of your mother's pieces—a ring, locket, bracelets and other small trinkets." She stopped her pacing for a moment and looked at me.

"So how long do I have to prepare?"

I paused dramatically, gave a sigh, and said, "Two weeks."

My pronouncement set off the predictable hysterics.

"You can't think that I can get all this done in such a short time!"

But she could and she would; she always managed, somehow, and she worked much better under a short timeline. Or at least that was my experience with her. I commiserated and assured her of my deep appreciation of all her efforts and the sleepless nights that were on the horizon. Kipp, meanwhile, was being a sponge and enjoying the interplay.

We took our leave and I returned to my studies of period manuscripts while Kipp went to find Juno. At the end of the day we met up, and Kipp, Lily and I started our walk home. Lily, although enjoying her time with Fitzhugh, who allowed her free run of his domain, was comforted to be reunited with Kipp. She had definitely imprinted on him, and even I could read the attachment in her little cat brain. The day had been long, and the shorter days of fall were beginning to shadow our walks home in twilight. There was some traffic so Kipp mentally instructed Lily to be on his right side, away from cars. She dutifully complied but was an impulsive creature, so we had to keep a watch on her.

Arriving home, I worked on a modest dinner for the three of us while Kipp chased Lily around the back yard. When they finally came in, Kipp indulgently let Lily position herself between his forepaws as they shared the chicken that was in his bowl. After it was polished off, Lily moved to her little bowl and finished that, too. She was going to be a round cat, I feared.

I, in the meantime, enjoyed hot vegetable soup. My preference was vegetarianism, but on most of my trips my choices were limited and a great deal of the food fare was often animal protein. Sometimes survival trumped personal preference. Technically I was in training and should have been focusing on healthy nutrition but could not pass up a bowl of ice cream. Kipp was naturally interested as he had not taken note of this food source previously.

"It's not good for your health," I commented, looking at his pleading eyes.

"You're eating it," he replied, exposing me for the total hypocrite that I was.

"Okay, just a little bit." I placed a scoop in his bowl and then a teaspoon full in Lily's. It was vanilla bean and I thought he was going to collapse with pleasure. Lily was pretty darn happy, too.

"You're going to have to run that off tomorrow. And Lily is getting too fat, Mother," I added, chiding Kipp.

After watching a little news on the television, we retired. Although it was getting cooler, I had not yet turned on any heat in the house. The resulting fact was that Kipp and Lily both piled on top of me, the three of us sharing our collective body heat. This close physical contact was not unusual for *symbionts* and, after all, Lily was a cat, one of the most comfort seeking creatures on earth. As we lay there relaxing, Kipp briefed me on his experiences with Juno, and I was complementary of their work. He was so modest, it was easy to overlook his preparations; mine were a bit more obvious and flashy.

Kipp had his muzzle on my chest, Lily resting on her back between his forepaws. He casually was cleaning her face and scored a droplet of ice cream that lingered on her chin, savoring the flavor for a moment when it registered on his tongue. She fell asleep almost immediately; her long days with Fitzhugh were carving out time from her needed sleep quotient.

"Petra, tell me some of your thoughts about the people we will encounter—some of their culture and history."

Where to start, I mused?

"Well, these colonists would have come from England. We could face an all male group or males and females living together, based on what we know from the other two Roanoke Island settlements. The people will have been chosen for their abilities to bring certain skills and knowledge to build a town. Most of them will probably be middle class and upper middle class; there will possibly be some gentry among them, keen to be the first on the continent, hoping they can acquire large tracts of land in return for their assistance in taming the wilderness. They will all be Christians, probably fairly religious and very socially conservative. If it is a mixed sex colony, the men will be totally in charge. I think the women will all be married and basically chattel with no power except through their influence on their husbands' decisions."

I paused for a moment and slightly shifted my legs which were cramping from too many squats at the gymnasium earlier that day.

"Kipp, I'll need you to be my alter ego, my conscience, to speak up when you see me making any tactical errors."

"Was that Tula's role with you?"

That was not what he wanted to ask me, but he was not immediately forthcoming. His lack of ease was unusual and even more so was his hesitance in sharing with me.

"Kipp, what's bothering you?"

He paused and then a rush of thoughts flew by so quickly that I could not find any one with which I could connect. Sensing my dilemma, he forced a slowing and subsequently formed one coherent thought.

"Juno told me that she thinks it is my obligation to have a child one day, so that I can pass on my genetics to another generation."

I was a bit startled and found myself feeling irritation with Juno, that she would place such a burden on him.

"Petra, have you ever had a baby?" His soft inquiry startled me out of my mood.

This was the one area of my life that I rarely discussed, but the relationship with a *symbiont* was so unique that there should be no area concealed, since the bond required intense depth of understanding of one another. All former events in one's life could influence behaviors in the present. The painful past welled up in me, and I unexpectedly felt as if I was about to cry. Kipp, of course, felt this, too, and tried to nestle even closer, if that was possible.

"It's okay, Kipp. It was a long time ago, but, yes, I did have a baby. He was a beautiful little boy named George." I paused for a moment to collect myself.

"He and his father were killed in an automobile accident," I added when I felt more composed.

"You never stop missing those that are loved, do you?" he asked, thinking briefly of his mother.

"No, you don't." After a few moments, I maneuvered the discussion back to Juno's suggestions about fatherhood.

"Why was Juno discussing babies with you?"

"She was commenting on some of my skills, which she says are unique; she felt that it was important they not be lost." He paused before asking, "How are relationships of that sort handled between *symbionts*? I asked Juno and she said that you would explain it all to me."

Oh, great, I thought. Juno left me with the big discussion about love, sex and relationships. Wasn't there a book or something to which I could refer him?

"Kipp, there are no hard and fast rules about this, but I can tell you from history and experience what is most successful, and then I'd trust you to make your own choices." He gave a soft grunt in the affirmative, and I continued.

"Relationships between *symbionts* are rather complicated. If you have a humanoid and a lupine that are bonded, as are you and I, they have developed a certain synergy that does not lend itself to other emotional entanglements. That's not true of *symbionts* that aren't in a bonded relationship for the purpose of time travel. They tend to conduct their private lives in a totally different manner. For example, Philo has been married for many years to a humanoid symbiont and has never bonded with a lupine. He is totally happy with that arrangement and has never missed any other aspect of our nature." I paused to consider how to continue, thinking that a discussion on quantum physics would be less complicated. Lily, fast asleep, was obviously in a dream state, twitching, her little legs kicking some imaginary prey.

"We like to think of ourselves as a highly moral, disciplined species," I continued, "but we are different from humans in that our primary relationships were originally meant to be with our *symbionts*. It's as if we have two sets of critical partnerships. One is with our *symbiont*, and remember that in our not so distant past, all *symbionts* had the innate ability to travel through time; the other is with a *symbiont* with whom we can procreate. For us, having children is very desirable on an emotional level and of course is critical for the survival of the species."

Kipp listened with rapt attention as I did my best to explain the extremely complex nature of it all. A bonded *symbiont* typically would form what might be described more as a partnership with another *symbiont* for the purposes of having children. This, too, would be a committed relationship, and all involved, humanoid and lupine, would share in the raising of the child.

"But as I said, there are no rules or laws about this. For instance, if you wanted to make your primary relationship with a female lupine, you could dissolve your bond with me and focus on her and creating a family. I've known of many humanoids that have done that, too, usually ones who either cannot travel or have given up that part of their lives. In the end, however, I would encourage you to do what is best for Kipp, and not do anything that Juno or I might tell you to do." I continued, "And that's because as much as we love you, we also have our own interests involved and therefore nothing we tell you can be completely of pure motives."

Kipp was quiet, and his rushing thoughts had slowed down considerably.

"I will think about all you have told me, Petra. But I do know one thing for certain: I don't want to leave you, and I do want to travel and work with you. There may be some time in my life that I want a child, but not now and not anytime soon."

I smiled at him.

"I think you would be a wonderful father, and the thought of us being up to our neck in little Kipps makes me feel happy."

"I don't know about that. Just keeping up with Lily has about finished me off. I can't imagine doing all this with a bunch of little ones." He laughed at the thought but then took a serious turn again.

"Petra, I know you still grieve over the loss of baby George, but will you ever consider having another baby?"

"Not now, and I really try not to think too much about it. I put all my energy into work and travel and for me that seems to work best." I felt uncomfortable talking about all this but finally added in a way of explanation, "Kipp, thinking about George literally cripples me, and as much as I have tried to heal and move on, I can't. So I just push it deep down and work, work, work."

I felt a tear escape my eye which Kipp gently licked from my cheek.

"It's alright with me, Petra. I won't ask you about it again."

With that, we fell into a deep and relaxed sleep. Maybe sharing some of my thoughts was beneficial, after all. Upon arising the following day, I found my gaze, as always, unconsciously wandering toward Tula's tattered blanket, which still lay in the corner of my bedroom. I had avoided dealing with that lingering remnant of her former existence. Kipp must have wondered if I would ever move it from its conspicuous location but had avoided broaching the issue. I suspected that in his wonderful way, he was being patient and letting me know he was not threatened by any old memories. Yes, that would be like Kipp.

Slowly, I sat back on the edge of the bed and dropped my head in my hands for a moment. Kipp, who had taken Lily outside, walked back in and caught me, unawares. Walking towards me, he placed his head on top of mine and embraced me, sharing my thoughts. I had to do this, I knew, and finally mustered enough courage to go to the dim corner and gather up Tula's blanket. It was all I had left of her. Pressing it to my face, I deeply inhaled her scent. Hesitating for a moment, I held it out for Kipp and he buried his nose in the wool, taking in what remained of Tula. It felt surprisingly good to share her with him.

With Kipp at my side, we went to the garden and, after retrieving a shovel from the shed, I dug a hole in the soft loam, breathing in deeply the scent of moist soil and rotting vegetation. After carefully folding the blanket, I placed it in the ground and covered it with the soft earth. Kipp wandered about the yard, and finding a stone, he brought it back and carefully placed it on the area, marking it. The symbolic closure felt good to me.

I left Kipp and Lily at that point and went back inside to make coffee. In disgust, I found I had absolutely no clean clothes and quickly threw a load in the washer. I was in serious need of a manager or someone to remind me what to do and when. We three had a small breakfast, and after a wait while my jeans dried, we began our morning walk towards Technicorps to begin the day. The morning was brisk and Kipp's fur was bristling in the cool air.

"Do you feel up to a longer walk?" I asked. Kipp was always ready to go the distance, and I had the carrier for Lily when she became fatigued. We zigzagged down several side streets until we were leaving habitation for the countryside. A little ahead of us, a graveyard stretched, the granite markers pocking the hillside in their somber display.

"What is this place?" Kipp asked.

"It is a cemetery, and humans bury their dead here. We, too, on occasion bury our dead here."

We walked over the small rise and I took Kipp to a granite marker.

"Here is where little George lies. I occasionally come to visit and sit with him. If you wish, you may come with me when I spend time with George. Tula didn't like it here. I think she felt helpless to fill that void that was left when he died, but, of course, I never expected that of her."

Kipp walked to the tombstone and carefully lay down,

his body pressing against the cold granite, muzzle down in the dew damp grass. I choked back emotion—Kipp was using his body to comfort George as he did me. We stayed like that for a while, keeping a careful eye on Lily who was off in exploration mode as she darted in and out of the tombstones, her tail arched high, ears back.

Part of me could have stayed all day since this was my first visit here since returning from my last time shift. But the sun was rising higher in the sky and the dew and mist were burning off in a reminder to me that I had obligations and responsibilities.

We arrived at Technicorps later than usual, chilled and damp, and the first thing we did was to take Lily down to Fitzhugh who kindly offered me a hot drink; there were times I envied Kipp's dense fur coat. Kipp took his leave to find Juno and I went to meet Suzanne. Kipp and I spent the day apart, but simultaneously we were working towards out upcoming journey. Juno's focus was helping Kipp learn how to react, stay safe, and perform optimally in the high risk situations found during time travel.

I found Suzanne in her customary frenetic mode, a pencil stuck in her unkempt hair, tape measure around her neck, shouting commands to her underlings. It was too much energy for me, so I left and returned to Fitzhugh's library and pulled some additional manuscripts on the lifestyles and customs of late 16th century England, as well as documents on the early colonization of America. I still had much role development to complete. Philo appeared in mid afternoon to check on my progress; his task was to report back to the Twelve. He seemed satisfied with my preparations and commented on Kipp's work with Juno in a highly complementary manner.

"Do you have a tentative date in mind?" he asked.

"I am aiming for October 20 and that will give me another two weeks. Well, at least that is what I told Suzanne to keep her motivated."

Philo laughed, understanding her style of work.

"Sounds good, so I will update the others. I thought your original goal was a little too optimistic and feel better that you are giving yourself more time to prepare." He stared at me for a moment, and then asked, "Something is bothering you; what's going on?"

He knew me too well, of course, so there was no need for me to avoid his questions.

"Juno has been talking with Kipp about having children one day. I had to have the much dreaded birds and bees discussion last night."

"Well, good for you," he said with a laugh. "But that is not what is hanging on to you, is it?"

"We buried Tula's blanket together," I offered, avoiding telling him the full story. I'm not sure why I would think that one telepath could fool another, especially when they were as close as Philo and I. At his frown, I finally added, "We talked about George, and I guess it just bothered me more than I would like."

Philo reached out and squeezed my arm.

"Sorry, Petra. But I think it was important you talk with Kipp, even though you will never share with anyone else. He does need to know; your survival might depend on it one day." He paused and smiled.

"Remember the time George disappeared and we couldn't find him? You were frantic and we tore the house apart, looked out in the garden, everywhere. Then we heard a chuckle and found him way in the back of your closet, hiding, with one of your big hats on his head. He looked so silly..." his voice trailed off.

I began to laugh, too, with the memory.

"Thanks, Philo. You reminded me of something important, and that is to balance the sadness with the good memories. And all my times with George were good."

He left me with a smile and I spent the remainder of the day with my head down, reading, until I felt my eyes would cross with the effort. At one point, I was startled to find Fitzhugh had soundlessly padded to my side, where he waited patiently to gain my attention.

"I have wanted to say something to you for a while now," he began awkwardly.

"I think I have maybe been too hard on you in many ways, and I regret that." He paused and added, "And I wanted to thank you for trusting Lily to my care while you are gone."

I looked at his aged face, wreathed in wrinkles, his long hair grey and untidy. He had always been an intimidating presence to me, and now here he was, vulnerable, exposing his usually hidden gentler side.

"Fitzhugh, I have been all the things of which you have accused me: reckless, hasty, and often unwilling to take direction when needed. So, you have done me a valuable service by telling me the truth. I would like to think that maybe I've grown some, thanks to you, Philo and Juno."

His eyes opened wider beneath his heavy brows.

"I wish you and Kipp well and know you will work together as a great team."

It was a surprise for me, this moment, but one I would think back on and cherish in the coming days. It could be cataloged as a nice end to a long day that had begun with grief and sadness.

CHAPTER 14

Juno sought me out a few days later, having left Kipp behind for some meditation and focused practice sessions. I had wandered out into the garden, much fatigued with books, reading, and work in general. It was mid October, my favorite time of year. The foliage, taking its cue from nature, had begun to assume its autumnal mantle and the cooling air was pleasantly crisp. The lichen covered bench beneath my familiar towering tulip poplar was a welcomed old friend, though the cool stone seat was bracing, even through the heavy fabric of my jeans. Sensing her thoughts, I knew Juno was searching for me, first in Fitzhugh's library and then the gym. I could visualize her, padding from one area to another, wanting to locate me but avoiding any intrusive characteristic to her pursuit. There was an "aha" moment as she finally found me, honing in on my life force.

"Hello, Petra," she greeted me in her gentle manner, physically coming into view. "I wanted to take some time and tell you of my work with Kipp. And he knows I am here," she added unnecessarily.

I remained quiet while she gathered her thoughts.

"I know you are familiar with the story of Pico. Did you ever meet him?"

"No, I never did. But of course I have heard of him. He

is legendary as one of the greatest *symbionts* of all time."

"Well, I did know him, and he was simply amazing, with a clarity of thought and purpose that was and still is exemplary. He led much of the revisionist work to reform our species in terms of ethics and purpose."

I was not sure where all of this was leading but contained my curiosity.

"I have worked with many *symbionts* in my long life," Juno continued, "but I have never met anyone like Kipp. He puts me in mind of Pico, with the exception that he is more focused, more talented, more...." her thoughts trailed off as she searched for the right word. "Pure, that's it; he is pure."

Juno took a couple of steps towards me until her head hovered over my knees. Having not been physically this close to her in a while, I was startled to see the opacity in her eyes; her muzzle was grizzled and it struck me that she was quite elderly. She rested her head on my lap and I gently caressed her ears.

"You are fatigued," I began, but she brushed off my concern.

"There is more I need to say to you, Petra. Kipp has touched me in a way I never thought possible. He has the capacity, simply because of who he is, to make one want to be better, to be more. When I am with him, I think of all that I could have been, my failings—I think he makes me feel humble. He has the ability to inspire us all." She paused momentarily before adding, "And you are taking on a great responsibility as his bonded *symbiont*. He needs someone who is ethical, who will help him always chose the right path. For all his great strengths, he is like a modeler's clay."

I was filled with self doubt.

"What if I'm not the right match for Kipp? He probably needs someone with more experience, more balance. You know me—rash, temperamental, or at least that's what the Twelve usually tell me."

Juno rested her head on my knee.

"Petra, the fact you did not seek him out and would give him up so easily means you are the perfect match for him. I don't fear you will mislead him in any way." She gave a soft grunt. "And despite everything else, he loves you completely and has fixed his affection and trust on you, and there is nothing to change that." She focused for a moment. "Even now, I can feel him gently reaching out for you."

"Juno, what have you told him about his enhanced abilities?"

"I told him that, unfortunately, we can't trust that everyone would understand or support his use of thought insertion. So I have counseled him to keep this private, at least for now. I also told him that this ability is natural and should be used, and that I would reserve it for extreme situations where life or death might be involved. I have every confidence that he will make the right choices, when called upon to do so."

She turned and slowly made her way across the garden; I noted a slight arthritic stiffness in her hind legs. I didn't know her exact age, but she was older than Philo, that much was evident. For all her years, however, her brightness was undimmed and she could outwork, outthink and outmaneuver any *symbiont* I knew.

The countdown to our departure to what I hoped would be a successful journey had begun. It was October 16 and we planned to leave on the 20th. As we walked home that evening, I decided that we would take the next day to play—no study, no meditation, just have fun. Following a sound night of rest, Kipp, Lily and I piled into my car and, after dashing through a local drive-through to pick up some really unhealthy food choices, we took off to Duke Forest. The weather was crisp, the ground dewy, and a subtle veil of mist covered the countryside. Parking my car, I unwrapped a steak egg and cheese biscuit for Kipp; he almost passed out in pleasure as he bit into the soft, warm food. Taking a second biscuit, I took the steak and pulled little pieces of it for the growing Lily to eat. The remainder of that one was mine, minus the meat. Kipp had polished his off and then tackled another.

"Humans have really developed some good tasting food," he commented.

"And much of it is really not good for us or them," I added. "But of course, that is what makes this fun."

After we finished off the breakfast fare, we disappeared into the forest. There was no one else apparent, so Kipp really stretched out, something he rarely had the opportunity to do. He was a thing of beauty as his fleet body moved low over the floor of the dense forest. Lily, likewise, was running but was no match for Kipp. I am not sure what happened to me, but before I knew it, I was running, too, the three of us acting like wild creatures—regressed and fundamental in the natural world.

We drew near to my glowing copse of trees. Winded, I slowed my running to an easy jog. The early morning light was just beginning to penetrate the dense foliage, stabbing here and there at the forest floor. The woods had the scent of early autumn, slightly musty, the leaves beginning their journey towards death in a spectacular display of color. Kipp unexpectedly startled a brood of mourning doves, nesting in a thicket. Their wings beat the air, the sound filling our ears, as they took flight. Lily had finally tired, so I placed her in the carrier. She had learned to curl herself inside, poking her little triangular face out of the open top.

Arriving at the copse, I seated myself on the familiar downed oak. Kipp, tongue hanging, dropped down on a bunch of dense ferns. We rested in silence for some time, listening to the ancient murmurings of the woods.

A sharp shriek penetrated the air; Kipp tilted his head a moment, then looked at me and said, "Somebody just found their breakfast—and it wasn't a steak biscuit."

"Can you always tell what has happened?" I asked.

"Usually I can, through my personal knowledge as a hunter, as well as my sense of smell." He paused for a second before remarking, "I've explained to Lily that we will be gone for a while. She wants to go with us, but I told her she will have to stay with Fitzhugh. Of course, she's fond of him, so she's not too disappointed."

Lily, in the meantime, had gone to sleep in the carrier, which I had gently placed in the ferns where Kipp relaxed.

"Juno and I talked yesterday about your work and your future." I hesitated a moment, unsure of what to say. "I hope I am up to the challenge of being your, well, mentor. I am significantly flawed, while you are quite honestly superior to me in most ways."

"Petra, we are a team and hopefully we compliment each other in all ways." His thoughts changed, and a veil of sadness appeared for a moment. "You know, after my mother died, I thought I would die, too—but of loneliness. I left our den and made my way northward, hoping I might one day find other *symbionts* with whom I could relate. But there were none to be found. I would, under cover of darkness, approach encampments of humans and listen to their voices. I even tried to join packs of wolves, but they were fearful, recognizing my alien nature, and rejected me. I knew there was no place for me there or anywhere on earth." He paused and with effort contained his sad memories. "But then one day, I heard your voice cry out, needing help, lonely as was I." He glanced up at me, his eyes bright. "I can't tell you how I felt that day. I ran, as fast as I was capable, until I found you—fearful if I didn't hurry that you would disappear like a fog bank, burned off by the morning light." He stood up and walked over to where I was seated.

"One glance at you—cold, exhausted, lying beside that pitiful fire—and I recognized my destiny was to be found there. All that showed of you beneath the elk hide was your face, pale, thin, your eyes telling me the story of your journey. Even though your appearance was different from mine, I recognized you immediately as being like me. My isolation, in that moment, had ended forever." Placing his head on my knee, he said, "We are as one now, be it good, bad or indifferent."

"It's just, Kipp, that I want to do right by you, if that makes sense."

Cocking his head to the side, he stared at me for a long moment before asking, "Well, why wouldn't you?"

"That is my point," I replied. "You lack deceit in your nature and therefore think everyone else is as honest and forthright as are you. But most of us are more complicated with conflicting agendas."

He laughed in response. "In case you didn't know, Petra, I was already aware you are not perfect. No surprise to me, at all." He paused and added, "But I love you anyway."

Stretching my neck back, I gazed up at the canopy of trees. There was a fleeting thought, the hope that all would go well and that one day the three of us would return to this place and enjoy it as we did today. Kipp's mind was made up, as Juno had observed, and that finished the discussion.

"I suppose that means we will finish our preparations and leave for the Land's Point Colony on October 20 as scheduled," I commented, keeping the tone of my thoughts purposefully light.

The next day, Kipp and I kept a scheduled meeting with Philo and Juno, who were acting as representatives of the Twelve. This was customary, close to departure, to review preparations to date and also to problem solve through particular situations that might occur. Philo and Juno kept up a rapid fire line of questions—the 'what if' situations—to see how we would respond, independently and as a team. Kipp's tendency was to defer to me, but they forced him to take the lead in many hypothetical situations. This lasted almost the entire day, and we stumbled home, completely exhausted, after ten hours. Even the normally energetic Kipp was depleted. I reassured him that this was the last time we would be expected to do this and that the next two days would be spent in very low key activities. Really, the only item left on my list was to retrieve my clothes and articles I would need from Suzanne.

The evening of October 19 was spent in a manner traditional for all traveling *symbionts*: a small group of friends gathered at my home to celebrate our upcoming journey. As had been done for hundreds of years, they all brought food, and we laughed, shared and enjoyed stories and memories. Philo and Juno were there, of course, along with Tom and Suzanne. Surprisingly, Fitzhugh came with the group—to my knowledge he had never attended a send off party. He might be softening up a little, I thought, but on the other hand, he was to take the silly one, Lily, and be her mother while we were gone. So it could, after all, be all about Lily and have little or nothing to do with me or Kipp.

Philo shared some stories about me, the majority of which left me thoroughly embarrassed; some were quite old, events I had not shared with Kipp.

"Oh, please don't share that tale," I pleaded, when he started one that I'd hoped would stay buried in the vault of time. I didn't know it then but realized later that he was trying to share another side of me with Kipp. After all, life wasn't meant to be totally serious; there was much joy and humor to be found.

After several hours, the party drew to a close. Fitzhugh, who had shared a ride with Tom, held Lily close as he departed. An anxious Kipp accompanied them outside, giving Lily a last damp nuzzle as her little triangular shaped face disappeared into the car.

"Don't worry, Kipp; you will see her again soon. I will take very good care of her," Fitzhugh said, with uncharacteristic gentleness in his voice.

Philo and Juno lingered after the others had left.

"Okay, now for the traditional words of wisdom," Philo began, with a soft laugh.

I rolled my eyes, and dropped on the sofa; Kipp came to my side and hopped up next to me, resting his head on my thigh.

"Petra, this is an extraordinarily dangerous trip. If you recall, I said that you and Tula wouldn't have been allowed to make this particular journey. You were, as I remember, rather miffed at my having said that, but Tula, for all her talents, did not have the abilities of Kipp." He seated himself. "We usually have more information about a culture, or a particular event in history, but this Land's Point colony is a total void. It might not even exist."

Philo rose and came over to squeeze next to me on the sofa. Putting his arm around me, I was smashed between him and Kipp. I relaxed my head on his shoulder; Juno approached and placed her muzzle on top of Kipp's head. We made a cluster of *symbionts,* and, for a while, words were not needed.

Finally, Philo gave a sigh.

"Petra, you will be the lead, since you have the experience. But Kipp, inexperienced though he is, is your superior in terms of skills. This journey will be a test for you both to learn how to balance one another. Successful *symbionts* are perfectly balanced. If I didn't believe you have that ability, I would never have permitted you to go."

Juno, who had been quiet, spoke up at that point.

"Kipp, your main task, on this your first journey, is to learn how to stay in character; remember, you are much like an actor. You have to mask your true identity in the presence of humans, while you are simultaneously communicating with Petra as a *symbiont.* This is difficult, and the purpose of all of our concentration exercises is evident: the successful *symbiont* is the one who has mastered concentration and self control."

They were lingering at this point, and I decided it was time to encourage them to leave, lest their anxieties become the focus of the evening.

"Not meaning to be rude, but Kipp and I need to get some sleep."

With that prompter, Philo and Juno said their good byes. I looked around the room, which was pretty overwhelming with the clutter of glasses, plates, and other remnants from the party.

"Is this customary?" Kipp asked, wondering why we had been abandoned to clean up duty.

I had to laugh.

"I have asked myself that many times. But, yes, as strange as it seems, it's part of the ceremony and is meant to be in fun." With that, I began to clear away the mess, carrying glasses to the kitchen sink. Kipp helped as much as he could, while lacking opposable thumbs. As was usual for me, I didn't stop with the party leftovers but began to give the entire house a fairly significant cleaning. It was something my mother had taught me: never leave home with it in disrepair. This was probably analogous to the human maxim of always wearing clean underwear in the event of an accident. It probably helped me work off my nervous energy, too. At one point, I rummaged through my rack of DVDs and found one of my favorites, *Jane Eyre*, the version with Orson Wells and Joan Fontaine. Kipp did not share my enjoyment of movies, given the fact he did not comprehend spoken language. The one dimensional media of television did not allow him to use his telepathic gifts. From time to time, he would ask me to explain what was happening. Picking up on my feelings during the movie, he honed in on the scene where Mr. Rochester tells Jane that his heart is tied to hers with a string, and if the string were to break he would be lost. I translated the scene and Kipp cocked his head sideways, staring at me.

"That's how I feel about you, Petra. If our string breaks, I will be adrift." He hopped up and wandered over to a large box sitting on a side table. "What's in here?" he asked.

I replied it was full of family photos, which one day I would catalogue if I could ever have a free moment.

"Show me," he said. With that, I dropped my dust rag and took the box to the center of the floor and sat down, cross legged, on the worn woven rug. Kipp padded over and plopped down at my side. Opening the box, I rifled through the pictures until I found an old one, a photo from the turn of the century.

"Here is my mother," I said, showing him the sepia toned version of my mother in Edwardian dress. It had been taken not long before her death, and despite her advanced years, her strength and humor still were evident.

Kipp looked from the photo to me.

"You look a lot like her," he commented. "What was she like?"

Taking a deep breath, I considered my reply.

"She was smart, funny, very driven, and sometimes impatient; she had a temper, but fortunately I rarely saw that side of her."

"Sounds like someone I know," Kipp commented mildly.

My hand trembled for a moment, and then I captured it: the baby picture of George, the one where I had bought him a sailor outfit and took him to a studio for a portrait. There was my little man, looking all serious, his chubby face staring at the camera, not certain if he wanted to laugh or cry. That day was as clear to me as if it had just happened yesterday.

"Baby George," Kipp's thoughts were even, still, like a gently flowing river stream. "He did not look like you, Petra."

"No, he looked a great deal like his father. And probably was more like him in temperament, too. Very easy going, happy, always laughing, being silly; he enjoyed life."

"Why do you keep this picture in a box? I would think

you would want it out where you can look at it from time to time." He paused and looked around the room. "In fact, you don't have any pictures displayed. Why is that?"

Hesitating, I responded lamely, "Well, I've meant to but just haven't done it yet."

It is impossible for bonded symbionts to be deceitful, so Kipp recognized my lie for what it was.

"No, you didn't. But rest assured, when we get back, I will make certain that the pictures are out so that we can enjoy them every day."

"Okay, bossy, whatever you say," I replied lightly, thinking he was probably right and knowing he would give me the push I sorely needed.

Finally, I climbed into bed, tired, but feeling excited and optimistic about the next day. Kipp took his place at my side, muzzle on my chest. My hand found its way to his head and I absently stroked the soft fur.

"I already miss Lily," he remarked. "It doesn't seem right not to have her mashed between us, making that strange noise you call a purr."

"Yes, and think of how rotten she has become and Fitzhugh having to manage her."

Kipp laughed at that and for a few minutes our thoughts tangled in mirth as we simultaneously pictured Fitzhugh chasing Lily up and down the stacks as he peeled her off of ancient binders and cleaned hair balls off the leather seat of his favorite chair. Within a few minutes, we were both in the land of nod.

CHAPTER 15

We slept late the next day, the dual consequences of a very late evening combined with the over stimulation of an excess of activity prior to bedtime. But there was really no need to rush, since we would be at our final destination in a flash of time. After awakening, I made us both a sizable breakfast, preparing our bodies for anticipated deprivation. Eating in silence, we were both actively working on marshalling our excitement with self control and meditative calm. I could feel Kipp's struggle with this task, but he was doing fine, as I reassured him. This was all unfamiliar territory for him—as a novice—but after a few days, he would be a confident pro.

Taking a cup of coffee to the small study that occupied the rear of the house, I took a seat at my desk and began to pay a few lingering bills. Even *symbionts* were burdened with onerous tasks. I always kept a current list for Philo, who managed my business until my return. Kipp trailed after me and finally gave voice to the disquiet within.

"I miss Lily," he remarked. "It doesn't seem normal not having to chase her from room to room, keeping her from trouble."

I had to laugh.

"I can see Fitzhugh running through the library...."

"I think he is too old to be a mother," Kipp commented. He dropped to the rug, curling up into a surprisingly tight ball, considering his size; the room was dark and cool. "Does this place remind you of the cave? All you need is a little fire and an elk skin." Kipp was in a pensive mood today.

"I would think you'd like it cool, since you are fuzzier than an old cave bear." We bantered lightly back and forth, mental jousting, both avoiding the mild anxiety which was an undercurrent. I did not say anything about it, having found this was always true and had been so prior to trips I would take with Tula—eager anticipation melded with frank anxiety.

"What will happen to Lily if we don't make it back?" Kipp queried, trying, but failing, to sound unconcerned. I was relieved he finally was able to ask that question. Our business was a high risk one.

"Kipp, we are doing very dangerous work. There's always a chance we won't return. If you think back, what were the odds I would have been able to come home after Tula was killed? Astronomical, but then you miraculously appeared." I paused and added, "If we don't survive, then Lily will live out her cat years, aggravating Fitzhugh, haunting the stacks of his library. And she will be okay; life will go on."

Kipp was quiet in response. I started to tell him that it wasn't too late for him to change his mind about the travel, but I knew that wasn't his intent. He had no true fear in him and was naturally of an inquisitive nature. Finishing up my business, we made our way to the bedroom, my intent being to stretch out comfortably and begin preparatory meditation. Kipp trailed after me, his soft padding audible on the worn wooden floors. The thick drapes were closed and the room was couched in twilight. The previous evening, I had laid out my period clothing, carefully assembled by Suzanne and her team. For me, this was almost ritualistic, like a knight donning armor, preparing for the looming battle. Fumbling a bit with the unfamiliar undergarments, I silently cursed and praised Suzanne; everything was created with attention to detail, to be sure. But in short order, I was clothed, with the small rolled pack of belongings that she had envisioned lying nearby. Kipp remained silent during all of this, watching me from his vantage point on the bed.

"Your top looks rather snug," he finally commented, having noted my struggle with the buttons of the weskit.

"I definitely prefer comfort and wish I could have worn sweats and tennis shoes, but I suspect that might have alarmed the colonists." I added, "I think I ate one too many egg and cheese biscuits lately."

Kipp laughed but commented, "I think you look very pretty."

Walking to the mirror, I gave myself a cursory glance. Plopping the wide brim hat that had been artificially weathered on my head, I observed where tendrils of my dark hair had escaped the confining braid to feather around my face. A small dusting of freckles were scattered across the bridge of my prominent nose. Hazel eyes stared back at me. Pretty? I did not think so, but vanity allowed me to enjoy his comment none the less.

"Petra, why are we departing from this location rather than the institute?" Kipp inquired. I was surprised this had not been discussed earlier, as a part of our history and experiences.

"Well, over time, we have tried different combinations of elements, and initiating the time shift from a very familiar, grounded location seems to work best. Our scientists have tried monitors of various types to see if they can lock down exactly what happens—physiologically speaking—during the shift." I had to stop and smile with humorous memories. "Once, they had Tula and me depart from the institute while they were monitoring our brain waves. I was targeted to arrive at the time of King Thutmose III and instead ended up in the midst of Akhenaton's rule. Of course, I had not been properly prepared for that time in history and it all quickly deteriorated. The whole event was a mess and required a very hasty and less than professional departure. As I recall, there was a lot of running and screaming involved."

Sitting down on the side of the bed, I began to breathe, deep and regular. After a while, I leaned back and lay down, as Kipp moved close to my side and placed his muzzle on my chest. Removing my hat, I clenched it against my side, along with my rolled pack. Kipp changed his focus to an internal one, the details of the room dropping away as he blocked all distractions from his notice; Juno had instructed him well. I felt the familiar contours of his mind as he gently invaded my thoughts. The experience is difficult to explain, but the expected boundaries that separate beings disappear, and two become one. Humans would find this dropping of barriers distasteful and terrifying; for us, it was as natural as breathing. It was an interesting sensation, moving through the time spectrum; there was an actual sense of physical motion that seemed directional. When coming forward in time, one experienced what felt to be the momentum of forward progression—rapid, to be sure, but progression none the less. Going back in time had just the opposite effect. As I lay on the bed, it felt as if I was slowly dropping backwards, falling through the mattress into a dark vortex; my body flexed, my head dropping towards my knees as I literally fell back in time. Kipp and I had mutually pooled our thoughts of the trip to Dare County and used the memories of physical sensations to ground us and help pinpoint our destination. Arriving at a near specific time was even more a challenge and required research, study and focus. Sometimes it worked, sometimes it failed. I found my ability to approximate the correct time had improved with years of practice.

Kipp, superior to me in all ways except experience, followed me into the void of time. We maintained awareness, although the fleeting disorientation we experienced was not unusual. I clenched his fur so tightly he emitted a slight whimper and pushed his muzzle against my breastbone to the point it caused pain. Yes, I reminded myself, we were still alive.

After what could have been seconds, minutes, days or weeks, the sense of movement slowed and eventually ended. My first thought was an awakening awareness of my situation: I was lying in a supine position, something sharp poking me in my lower back. Opening my eyes, I looked up to find myself surrounded by a canopy of deciduous trees—a dense forest loomed overhead. The sun was directly above, indicating the noon hour; its life giving light filtered through leaves that were touched with a tentative hint of autumnal color. The air was mild and pleasant and whether it was my imagination or not, it seemed to smell cleaner than the modern day version. I dug under my back and removed the offending stick. My other hand found the curve of Kipp's head, still resting across my chest, quiet, but he was beginning to stir, too.

"Are you okay, Petra?" he asked, raising his head slightly to look at me.

"Yes, and you?" I leaned up on my elbows and gazed about, still struggling to get my bearings. "What do you glean from your senses?"

He staggered to his feet, and, after a good, head clearing shake, he stretched his body thoroughly and then sat to regard our surroundings.

"The smell of salt air is strongest in that direction," he indicated, looking over my right shoulder. "And I get the scent of wood smoke, a fire burning, a short distance away," he said, indicating a ninety degrees trajectory. "And, yes, I detect humans and not too far distance from here."

"Do you have any impressions that would help identify if the humans are English settlers or Native Americans?"

Kipp closed his eyes and focused. I followed his thoughts and was amazed at the computer-like processing which was much too rapid and complex for me to follow.

"From the content of their thoughts, which are extremely remote and vague, I think they are settlers." He paused and I could detect confusion. "But the overwhelming sense I get is one of extreme fear that seems to override every thing else." He looked at me, puzzled. "What would make these people so afraid?"

I ignored his question.

"Do you sense anything else out there?"

He was quiet again, as he closed his eyes and turned his focus in a 360 degree scan, this lasted for several minutes as he took his time.

"Petra, I find this confusing. There is nothing out there, and I mean nothing—no wildlife, with the exception of birds and very small mammals. There are no deer or large predators, and I don't read any other people. What would they be so fearful of? I can't detect any threats."

I asked Kipp to stop his canvassing so that I could use my lesser skills. Throwing out my own net, I, too, immediately was hit full force with the collective fear of multiple humans. This was shocking to me, and quite frankly in my long career, I had never felt anything to compare. At this distance, there was no ability to actually discern individual thoughts, but the pervasive anxiety and terror was almost like an impenetrable wall.

Kipp stared at me, deferential, waiting for my lead, since my experience was the guiding force.

"What I would like to do is to walk away from where we think the colony might be, making a large circle to get a better sense of the land. Maybe we are missing something, and I don't want us to be caught unawares." Kipp acknowledged his acceptance of the plan, and, after regaining our footing, we began slowly walking in a northwestern direction.

We were far enough inland that the forest was thick and didn't have that stunted, beaten appearance that one often finds on the actual coastline. I identified several species that could be used by humans: slippery elm, witch hazel, and black cherry, as well as the staple of oaks and maples. Based on the color of the foliage as well as the air temperature, I determined that we had appeared in mid October. After a two mile trek inland, we swung to the east, making a large sweep. Kipp was still unable, as was I, to detect any humans, other than the original hit he had made. The land was level, gently sloping from the coast line, the soil a mixture of sandy loam and rotting vegetation. I filled my lungs deeply, enjoying the truly clean air, something lost in the twentieth century. We completed the leg of an imaginary triangle, still with no evidence of life, before turning back towards the coast, moving towards the collection of fearful humans we detected.

"How many people do you think are here?" I asked, watching as Kipp's ears continued to swivel to and fro.

"Not the hundred plus that were at the other colonies. It is hard to tell—maybe twenty or thirty. And I think there are both males and females here."

"Well, we already know something about the colony: they have had a massive loss of their people, either through death or migration. There is no way that England would have funded and established a colony of that few numbers. There always has to be a minimal amount of manpower for a group to be self sustaining."

We paused near a clear stream and sat for a few minutes to rest. I unrolled my pack and pulled out some dried fruit for me, along with a handful of nuts; for Kipp, I had dried jerky. Dipping our heads, we drank from the stream, the water cool and fresh. Kipp's head jerked suddenly up and he looked over his shoulder. I felt his alarm but did not detect anything. In that instant, the comforting forest sounds of birds murmuring ceased, and the wind picked up momentarily. Kipp's nostrils quivered as he accessed his more fundamental repertoire of senses to assess our environment.

"What is it?" I asked.

"I'm not sure; there was something there just for a minute, but now it is gone." He went on to address my more pertinent question. "I don't know if it was human or not but it was definitely something organic. I'm just not sure." His thoughts trailed off as he continued to focus his gaze into the dense woods. I noted that his auburn coat had brushed erect, an instinctive reaction. Putting my hand out, I gently smoothed his fur, trying to settle both of us for the moment. I confess, seeing Kipp's response caused a ripple of anxiety in me, too.

We sat there for a while longer, quiet, finishing the rest of our snack. There was no further disruption to our peaceful interlude. Finally, we got to our feet and continued in the direction of the coast, towards the human signals. Kipp walked to my right, slightly ahead, his shoulder pressing against my leg. He had unconsciously taken up a defensive and protective posture. My hand dropped down to ruffle his ears.

"We'll be okay." I reassured both him and myself.

As we kept moving, the sun overhead, which had done an admirable job of illuminating our path through the dense forest, suddenly darted behind a bank of clouds, thrusting us into dimness. Simultaneously, the wind picked up and the forest began to fill with sounds of trees moaning as they bent to and fro, their limbs scraping one another, leaves rattling and underbrush in movement. This caused more unease on our part, exacerbated by Kipp's sense that something unidentifiable had been close by earlier.

Placing my hand lightly on Kipp's back, I asked, "Nothing out there, right? I mean no big bugger bears or bigfoot?" I was trying to add some levity to the situation, for I had to admit that the fearful tone of the colonists, in addition to Kipp's radar hit, had caused me to feel nervous.

Kipp slowed his gait and sat. Carefully he swiveled his head and obviously was surveying the surrounding woods.

"Kipp, I was just kidding," I said.

"No, you weren't. You are anxious, and so am I."

"What do you think that was earlier that you detected?"

"I don't know. It felt, well...." he trailed off searching for a description. "I think the best description would be malignant. But," he added, "I don't even know if it was human or not."

"Somehow that is not comforting, Kipp."

"Don't worry, Petra. If something comes at us, I'll bite it for you with my big teeth." He glanced at me. "Seriously, we'll be okay."

Our roles had reversed. Kipp was the master and I the student, it seemed. And that was completely okay with me.

CHAPTER 16

The human footprint became more evident the further we walked. I was still disturbed by the powerful undercurrent of fear, but we had a job to do and were not in a position to just pack up and go home. Just ahead, I viewed a clearing and the outlines of a timber barricade.

"Alright, Kipp. We're here, and it's time to put on your game face. Assume your character and stay focused." He, in reply, nuzzled my hand and pushed his shoulder against my leg.

I changed my pace, walking slowly, trying to appear fatigued and stressed. Suddenly, there was a human voice, shouting an alarm up ahead, and then multiple voices joined in an anxious chorus.

"Hold there," a man called. "Do not advance."

"Please help me," I called back, having decided to use a modified English accent, wanting it to sound as if it had been influenced by years of travel as well as a dual nationality. Having acquired a fairly large repertoire of languages and dialects over hundreds of years of travel and work, I had the ability to change my presentation at will. But English was obviously the most appropriate, given with whom I would be speaking. We stood there, Kipp and I, waiting, until the humans could decide what to do with us.

Kipp was fully engaged and remarked, "Petra, they are still very fearful, but it is not directed necessarily at us, although they are cautious. We're perplexing to them."

Finally, a heavy wooden gateway was pulled back and several men stepped forward, slowly and with exaggerated care. One man walked a pace ahead of the others and appeared to be the de-facto leader. Reading their thoughts, I could tell they deferred to him, to some minor degree, but I did not think he was the natural leader. The man was of medium height, average build, with sandy colored hair and pale blue, close set eyes. He, as were the others, was wearing a shirt of rough woven wool, worn breeches, and all were armed with muskets.

"Who are you and what are you doing here?" he asked, darting his eyes past me to look into the darkening woods. His thoughts were clear to me: he was worried that I was part of some sort of assault party, sent in to distract them in advance of a planned attack.

"Sir, I am so grateful to you. Please help me." I did my best to sound vulnerable, pitiful, and pleading.

"Where is the rest of your party?" he queried, now looking at both me and Kipp more intently.

"Sir, my name is Petra Mendez Howard. I was on my father's ship, off the coast, when it hit the shoals and sank." I paused dramatically for a moment choosing my timing before adding, "I am the only survivor."

It was clear he did not believe me; he signaled for the men, in groups of two, to conduct a survey of the woods, no doubt to look for other members of my party. The fear that we had detected was still evident, but it was apparent that it was not directed towards me or any mythical landing party of aggressive Spaniards. The men looked at one another, hesitant to leave the barricade, but gripping their weapons, they paired off and disappeared from view into the gloaming.

The settler stared at me thoughtfully before asking, "Mendez? What sort of name is that?"

The moment had arrived—could I make this sound

plausible? Before I could respond, a duo of women approached, one of them flanking the man and lightly touching his shoulder with a pale and delicate hand. His wife, it seemed. Another woman, tall, spare, just this side of middle age, stood next to her. I immediately was drawn to her face, which was careworn, but one of those open faces that felt welcoming.

The settler's wife queried, "Richard, have you not introduced yourself yet?" Her tone was gently and cautiously chiding.

His irritation was evident, but he replied, looking at me, "I am Richard Waite; this is my wife, Mary, and this," he indicated the tall woman, "is Perdy James." The three of them stood waiting on me.

"Greetings," I said, nodding my head at the women. "As I said, I am Petra Mendez Howard, and my father's ship was lost off the coast. I am the only survivor." I repeated myself for the benefit of the women, who were less cautious and more sympathetic to me. Mary murmured her concern and started to walk forward, but her husband caught her arm.

"Mendez sounds to be a Spanish name," he began again. Well, it was time to launch my story and see how convincing I could be.

"Master Waite, my father was of Spanish origin. But he met my mother, and after they were married, in deference to her sentiments, he allied himself with England. He was a trader who sailed all over the world in search of exotic fabrics, spices, foods, and other marketable goods." I paused for a moment as the other men returned to hear my story. I would take a risk, betting that Richard Waite had a fragile ego. "Certainly, sir, a man of your knowledge and stature would have heard of my father. His name was Hector Mendez, and his ship was well known in London—she was the *Rose of York*."

The others looked at Waite, deferentially giving him time to reply. Of course, Kipp and I knew that he was searching frantically for the right response, wanting to look like an authority but having no clue about the mythical *Rose of York*.

"Why, of course, I have heard of the ship and your father." He did what I had anticipated: he inflated his human ego. He glanced around at the others, "Have not you heard of this man?"

One of the men even one upped him by murmuring that he had met Captain Mendez once at a reception in London, going on to mention what a fine man he was. This seemed to seal the deal—they were confident in the corroboration of the nonexistent facts. It was like the rumor that starts at one end of the room and, after it is passed from person to person, eventually becomes reality.

"So how did you become the sole survivor?" Mary Waite queried, her voice meek and soft spoken. She was possessed of a pretty countenance, with flaxen hair pulled back from an oval face and tied at the nape of her neck with a ribbon. At first glance, she appeared to be several years younger than her spouse. I noted that her husband had a flash of intense irritation that she would speak up without his permission. He would speak to her about this in private, later. I would have to be cautious of my prematurely negative reaction to him, since he appeared to be the power broker in this little pond.

"Mistress Waite, my father had heard of the colonies established here in the New World. We departed the West Indies after having taken on a cargo of spices, dried fruits, seeds for planting, as well as other commodities. He decided to sail along the coastline, wanting to seek out the colonies and effort trade and support." I paused for a moment, working up to an emotional display. Kipp was monitoring me with humor in his thoughts.

"And then, Mistress, we hit a shoal; the ship took on water and despite my father's attempts to shore up the hold, the ship began to sink, rapidly. He forced me to the departure boat and had the bosun's mate assist me."

At this point, I began to cry, for dramatic effect. Mary Waite was a kind, generous soul, this I could already tell, with no artifice in her nature; she walked forward and took my arm. If I were human, such artful manipulation of emotions should have been shameful; but I was a *symbiont* and manipulation was a tool of the trade.

"As the boat was lowered, the ship lurched starboard. The mate, a young man named Charlie, fell overboard and was crushed between the vessels. I drifted off after that, watching my father's ship go down, helpless. All I had for comfort was my dog, Kipp." At that, I ruffled Kipp's fur, and he wagged his tail and lolled his tongue out, trying to look very passive, stupid and happy.

I stopped my story, waiting for the group to respond. The general tenor of the group was one of mild anxiety directed towards me and Kipp, but they were still grossly fearful of something or someone else. It was as if their worry was so great over this other unnamed entity that I fell beneath the radar. Finally Waite spoke up and broke the impasse.

"It is getting late, and we need to secure our barricade for the night." He paused, and then glanced at me with his pale eyes. I was startled to read his thoughts: a flash of desire, red hot, sparked through him, and his thoughts towards me became suddenly and uncomfortably sexual. Of course, Kipp was aware of this, too, and communicated his annoyance to me. Waite continued, "You may stay with me and Mary."

That was not going to work, I thought, not wanting to be consumed with fighting off this sexually frustrated man. It appeared, however, that someone else would take care of this issue for me. Perdy, who had stood silent during all of the previous exchanges, stepped forward at that point.

"My house is empty, and I would welcome the company." Her words were mild but her thoughts were not. I was startled to read intense anger, almost to the point of hatred, directed at Richard Waite. I glanced back at Waite who was still staring at me, his thoughts primitive and aggressive. He was not appreciative at all with what he thought to be her interference in the matter but was struggling with what to say next lest he appear churlish. His standing as a leader was no doubt a primary concern of his.

"Kipp, I told you my bodice was too tight," I communicated silently, trying to inject some humor into the uncomfortable situation as we waited to see who would prevail. Kipp responded by wanting to know if I would like him to bite Waite on the buttocks.

"Petra," he was thinking, "why is Perdy so enraged at Waite? Do you understand what is going on?"

I replied in the negative; we had too little information at this point to draw logical conclusions. With that, I decided to take control of my destiny and stepped forward to touch Perdy lightly on the arm.

"Thank you for your kind offer; I very much would like to accept. Will my beloved Kipp be welcomed, too?" Before she could answer, I added that he was well behaved.

"Your dog can come, but we will not have food for him," she replied hesitantly. I knew she was trying to not be rude but necessity forced candor. These people were highly stressed and apparently food stores were low, adding to whatever was causing their grief.

"Not to worry, Mistress Perdy. Kipp can hunt and provide for himself," I commented.

One of the men spoke up and remarked that there was very little animal life in the area, making hunting difficult. I asked what had they been eating and was told that their main sustenance was fish, some turtles and the occasional beaver caught in the nearby river. This seemed odd to me that there seemed to be a gross shortage of deer and other larger animals, but this validated what Kipp had noticed earlier.

Waite spoke up, stating it was time to close the barricade for the night. At that very comment, the intense fear that had ebbed a bit in lieu of everyone's curiosity about me returned with a vengeance. I was not skilled enough to sort out individual thoughts in this tangle of overwhelming feeling but knew Kipp probably could. The men rolled the gate back in front of the entrance to the compound, effectively locking us all in for the evening. Perdy, her hand gentle on my arm, walked me towards her small cabin, a wooden edifice constructed of roughly hewn timber logs, the mortar made of mud and straw. The cabin shared three common walls with other like dwellings, a clever way to maximize living space with minimal resources and effort. These people had envisioned town houses long before the rest of us would.

I entered to find a sparsely appointed cabin, the ceiling low, forcing the tall Perdy to stoop just a bit when crossing the threshold. There was one small communal room where cooking and socializing was done and another adjoining room where one slept. A large, cast iron pot containing some sort of stew was hanging over the fully engaged fire that was blazing in the fireplace.

"There are so few of us that we take turns preparing meals for the community. I am making a fish stew which shall be taken to the hall for all to share; there are several other women, and we do most of the food preparation."

This woman was filled with sorrow and an atmosphere of extreme fatigue surrounded her in an oppressive display. A female would not have come alone to the New World, so I could only assume that her family had died from accident or illness or had been killed. After spooning out a meager serving for both of us, she excused herself and took the steaming pot to the communal gathering spot. She brought back something, not bread, but it was made of corn and nuts and had been mashed, baked and made into a hard crust to dip in the stew. As evidence of her kind nature, she also carried back a bowl with some of the excess stew, explaining that since there was a little left uneaten, she brought the remainder to Kipp.

Sitting across from me at her rough table, she bowed her head and said a prayer to bless our meal. Kipp had settled down on the hard packed dirt in front of the fireplace, where he watched all of this with curiosity. I knew he was reading her every thought. The food was barely palatable, and I swallowed with effort. The stew tasted mildly rancid and the corn planks just about broke out an incisor. Kipp, on the other hand, happily lapped his down, thinking it was marvelous.

Perdy looked up at me, anxiously remarking, "I hope it is to your liking." I smiled in reply and told her how grateful I was for her hospitality.

"My house has been empty for a while, so it is nice for me to have someone with whom to share a meal," she added with sincerity.

As her head lowered to slowly consume the stew, I cast a surreptitious glance at her. Her face was lined, prematurely, from exposure to the elements as well as worry. She had brown eyes, dark orbs that were fathomless. Her hair was abundant, but she had tamed it with effort, pulling it back severely from an angular face. By no means could she be called attractive, but there was something compelling about her, a quiet strength which was evident whether she was speaking or silent. Her clothes were plain and she had taken no extra care with her appearance; whereas Mary's hair was tied with a pretty piece of ribbon, Perdy had used a scrap piece of fabric.

We sat there, in quiet companionship, the crackling of the open fire the only sound to be heard. Kipp, however, was busy speaking to me.

"Her husband and her sister, someone named Nell, are both dead. He struggled for a moment, and then he added, "They died of a disease, something that moved through this camp quickly, killing a large number of the settlers."

Perdy's voice cut into my silent exchange with Kipp.

"We are at the last of our stores of corn, and we will be forced to forage further out in the forests for nuts and roots." As she said this, her unease peaked, again, and she nervously looked up, unconsciously toward the door of her little dwelling. I think she kept talking, more out of her anxiety than anything else.

"When we first settled here, we engaged in barter and trade with the local natives, many of whom were marginally friendly." She paused for a moment, and I saw her hands clench. "But they have abandoned this land and with them went our corn."

I wanted to ask questions but was not certain enough of the culture to know if I would be viewed as rude or vulgar. Past experience had taught me that being excessively inquisitive tended to make people suspicious. Kipp was counseling me to be patient, wait for the proper opportunity. I was grateful to have my balancing wheel.

Finally, I compromised with a murmured, "It must have been very difficult for you all."

"We had planted some crops," Perdy began, "but between the drought and other factors, we have had a very poor harvest."

Other factors? Now what had she meant by that? And when she said it, her anxiety peaked again, almost to the point of panic. I glanced at Kipp, who had stretched out on his side next to the fire and, although appeared asleep, was in actuality active and alert. He gave me the mental equivalent of a shoulder shrug; he had no idea about what was going on here, either. Perdy interrupted my thoughts.

"My home is quite small. You are welcome to share my bed, or if you prefer, we can prepare you a place to sleep here before the fire; it seems your dog likes it there."

I told her that Kipp and I would be very comfortable at the fireplace. After excusing herself for a moment, she left the cabin and shortly after returned carrying a rolled thin cotton mattress, stuffed with something, probably corn husks. She also had a quilt tucked under her arm. After one more trip, she brought some dried rushes which she scattered over the dirt floor; the thin mattress was placed on top of the rushes. All in all, it made a cozy place for rest.

Asking if I could help, she directed me to gather a few pieces of firewood from the rack outside. Exiting the door along with Kipp, who needed to relieve himself, I gazed across the compound. There was little activity; most of the settlers had gone in for the night. The area was basically a large rectangle, with corner guard posts at each angle. All four were inhabited, this in a land where the native population had abandoned the territory. The entire picture was a puzzle.

As I gathered a few pieces of wood, I became aware of an unpleasant prickling on the back of my neck, as if my flesh was crawling. Startled, I glanced up to see Waite across the compound, staring silently at me. His thoughts, venal and obscene, were obvious to me, but I noted with curiosity that he suppressed these with effort. I suppose some modicum of decency was present; he merely nodded his head in acknowledgement and turned away. Kipp trotted up, irritated, and again inquired if I wanted him to sink his impressive teeth in a portion of Waite's flesh. Laughing, I replied in the negative, assuring him that I could take care of myself and didn't need my honor defended. We made our way back to the warmth of Perdy's small cabin.

She thanked me for the wood and generously stoked the fire so that it would burn most of the night. After she excused herself to her bed, I removed my clothes down to my chemise and curled up on the thin mattress. Kipp crawled up next to me and curled up, his head on my chest.

After a moment of thought, he commented, "These people are obviously struggling to survive. They seem brave and tough to have taken on all this adversity, what with the drought, their inability to grow food and, most of all, the loss of so many dear to them from disease." He paused, gathering his thoughts. "But these courageous people are almost immobilized by some unknown fear. Petra, we must find out what it is, for that is the focal point of this mystery." I was cautious to remind myself to keep all of my communication with Kipp silent, lest anyone overhear and think me mad or possessed with demonic gifts.

"As you told me, Kipp, we must stay patient and let these people give information as they choose. If I get too pushy, they might become suspicious." A pale, flickering light illuminated the doorway to Perdy's room; she stood there, holding an oil lantern.

"Is everything suitable, Mistress Petra?"

"Please, just call me Petra. And, yes, thank you, I am very comfortable."

She smiled and remarked, "Your beastie, the dog, seems comfortable, too." After a moment, she added, "I had a dog once, but a small one. She often slept on the foot of my bed. I had to leave her behind in England when I came here." Her sadness was almost overwhelming in the confines of the tiny room.

I decided to take a chance and asked, "Mistress Perdy, how is it you have come to be alone here?" I could see her lower lip tremble a little and read her mental strain to keep her emotions in check.

"I came with my husband, Matthew; my sister, Nell, and her husband came, too. They all died of the typhoid that ravaged this camp." She took a deep breath and looked down at her clenched hands. "Of the 115 people who came here, 78 died of the fever. Since then, others have been lost, too." She closed up at that point, struggling with her internal dialog which counseled her to be silent.

I decided at that point to pull back telepathically as well as in my interactions and remarked, "I am so sorry for your losses, Mistress Perdy." There was always a balance of curiosity and compassion that was needed in an instance such as this.

"Well, you know what it is like, having just lost your father." I had a minor pang of guilt for lying with such ease, but then remembered little George, and realized that I, too, had suffered pain—so had Kipp. With wishes that I might rest well, she retired, leaving me and Kipp. We were exhausted from both our physical exertions as well as the mental ones and quickly fell into a dreamless sleep, my hand curled over the dome of Kipp's soft head.

CHAPTER 17

Breakfast the next morning consisted of dried, salted fish, accompanied by the dreaded corn planks. I privately took an oath to in the future avoid corn, granola bars—well, just about anything that even remotely resembled hard packed grains, seeds or nuts. Kipp, on the other hand, enjoyed the good teeth cleaning achieved by crunching on the planks. There was some hot tea, however, weak and without sugar—but still welcomed. I had found from years of travelling, that such deprivation always made me more grateful for the land (and time) of plenty in which I resided. My needs were few, so I took little, making certain that I would not cause the generous Perdy to lower her stores significantly. Kipp would forage later.

"Did you rest well, Petra?" Perdy's question interrupted my reverie. I replied in the affirmative and asked how I could be of help to her. "We will be going out into the forest today, looking for nuts, roots and any leftover fruits that might have dried on the vines. You can come with me and assist us, if you would like."

In short order, we were ready to go, and, after meeting up with several other women and an accompaniment of armed men, we left the stockade and began the long walk through the forest. The vigorous mix of deciduous and conifer trees that surrounded us acted in concert to block out the bright light of the sun, thrusting us into a cool, dim world. The ever present group anxiety traveled with us, hovering like a fog bank. I asked Kipp to casually make some large laps of the area and see what he could find. As we trudged along, we came to a clearing and what appeared to be a small field; it was scorched, and whatever had grown there had burned to the ground. I looked up at Perdy, the question clearly on my face. Her deep set dark eyes tried to avoid mine, but she finally seemed compelled to respond.

"We worked hard to plant some food, using seeds we brought from England as well as the corn we obtained in trade with the natives who once resided to the northwest." She paused, glancing around at the others who studiously avoided eye contact. "There was a fire and all was lost," she finally explained. Her mind was busy working, hoping I would not ask any more questions.

The thoughts of all the women were tightly shuttered, but I knew the fire was no accident. One of the ladies, a tiny, gentle soul named Alice, let her thoughts betray her placid exterior for a brief moment. I caught a glimpse of horror, the fear of an unnamed entity in the woods—what she envisioned to be a demonic spirit. Before I could glean additional bits, she slammed shut her mental door with a mighty effort. My assumption at this point was that these people, collectively, had made a decision to not discuss the obvious issue of whatever resided in yon forest. Beyond that, they were all so terrified, that their minds shut down in an act of suppression in order to keep functioning. I would need to tread slowly and carefully.

In the meantime, Kipp disappeared from view but remained in contact and had ranged some 200 yards, traveling over a small hillock to the northeast. He broke off for a moment as he honed in on a hapless rabbit which was efficiently dispatched and enjoyed for breakfast. I was pleased to be left out of that exchange. After a while, he trotted back to rejoin our group.

"I haven't seen anything," he commented, still licking his lips.

"Why don't you stay close by as we gather nuts? Act bored, unconcerned, maybe stretch out in a patch of sun but be scanning our perimeter." I told him of the tiny glimpse I had into Alice's mind. "I think there's something out here—something real, not a demon—but something they have distorted. But whatever it is, it burned down their field and ruined their crops. It's a vindictive son of a bitch." After a moment, I apologized for the vulgarity, since Kipp was literally speaking a son of a bitch, but he had taken no offense.

We finally reached our destination and began to collect acorns and black walnuts off the floor of the forest, placing them in woven baskets. The two men took up positions at either side of our group, facing outward, scanning the woods constantly, muskets leveled at the ready. Their caution seemed a little overdone to me. Surely we could see anything approaching our group in time to mount a defense. There were fleeting thoughts that indicated false bravado from the men. They were terrified, that much was clear, but their minds were filled with gallant, challenging threats as they stared out into the tangled underbrush.

After about an hour of gathering, I took a seat on the trunk of a fallen tree. Even though the air was crisp, I had worked up a sweat and pulled off my scarf to wipe my forehead. I happened to be facing away from the others and glancing up saw movement within a grove of tightly bunched American beeches probably 150 yards away; something large and stealthy was moving carefully just within the range of my vision. Due to years and years of hazardous work, I wasn't one to be easily frightened, but I'll admit, I felt the hair rise on the back of my neck. Kipp, who had lapsed in his attention for a moment, snapped to it when he felt my alarm.

Disciplined, however, he didn't start, but kept his lazy attitude while reclining on a bed of dead leaves; his mind reached out to the being we sought.

"What is it?" I asked, averting my eyes so that I would not appear to be so obviously staring.

Kipp's eyes were closed tight in concentration.

"I'm not sure; I've never felt anything like this. I would say it is human, but its mind is filled with confusion, conflict, hatred—animalistic type of thoughts. It wants to kill, destroy." He paused and took a deep, shuddering breath. "It makes me feel bad to read its thoughts."

"Pull back for a moment, Kipp, and gather yourself." I reached down and ran my hand along his flank; he needed grounding. With his disciplined mind, he managed to internalize and self contain his probing mind. Doing a quick visual scan, it seemed that the being or entity had fallen from sight. I was relieved the settlers had not seen it, as the cacophony of agitated thoughts would have compromised our abilities to assess. I focused my mind in the general direction of our target. There was a life force, retreating, so the imprints it was leaving were like tracks left in a melting snow bank. But what I could read was disturbing: there were aspects of humanity and animal, it seemed, somehow melded into one being. Definitely in my experience, this was totally unique. Perdy approached us, her step soft in the tangled undergrowth and fallen leaves.

"Is all well with you, Petra?" There was no accusatory tone as in the vein of shouldn't I be working instead of sitting.

"Yes, thank you, I am fine. I became heated and sat for a moment." My mind was working quickly now, as I wanted to get to that grove of trees where we had seen our silent watcher, hoping I could pick up some clues. "Perdy, I need to excuse myself, please, to take care of my needs."

"One of the men will accompany you...."

I interrupted her, remarking with ease, "That will not

be needed. I have my Kipp and trust he can look out for me."

She experienced the spike of terror, the likes of which I was now familiar in all of these people. Alice and Mary joined us and, for a moment, they seemed as if they were going to refuse my request and force a guard on me. Kipp took that moment to slowly stand, stretch and yawn, displaying his set of very large teeth. Of course, this was purposeful, and he finalized the moment by seating himself at my feet, his head reaching my lower chest. A tall lupine was he, impressive by anyone's standards. After that, the ladies demurred and entered no further objections.

They returned to work while Kipp and I made our way to the ridge. I was not fearful, since we both had the ability to detect any thought patterns ahead, and the grove to which we traveled was decidedly absent of life. The landscape was peaceful, with a bright sun lazily suspended high overhead, its rays making their way to illuminate the dense forest floor. I tried to walk quietly, but the leaves and branches were crunching under my feet; I lacked Perdy's skill in being a stealthy woods person.

After gaining the ridge, Kipp put his nose to the ground and began energetically working the area. I was pretty useless but walked along looking for any imprints in the soft soil. There was so much covering debris that it was difficult; I did see a couple of vague imprints, but they were of no significance to me except to suggest that something organic had traversed this area. No wraith, no demon, no spirit, I told myself.

"Petra, come here," Kipp called, excitement in his attitude. As I rushed to his side, he indicated a small tuft of grayish fur lying on the fallen leaves. Pushing his nose down, he examined the hair and exclaimed, "This is wolf."

"Are you sure?" I asked. "You know the settlers said there were no predators left in this area."

"I am very familiar with wolf, and this is wolf, definitely. But I also smell something else; I smell human here, too, where these indentations are in the ground." He indicated faint footprints, something made by a soft soled foot covering.

I asked if he could follow the trail and he indicated yes. After I instructed him to be careful, he wandered off, away from our harvesting location. Of course, I had to return to the settlers, lest they become suspicious. Kipp's thoughts became fainter with distance, but he relayed a comforting message that he was safe, from time to time. The sun was beginning to drift towards the western horizon, and Perdy signaled it was time to start back for the stockade. I was hesitant to leave without Kipp, but knew they would not leave me behind, so I walked with them, lagging to the rear, calling out to Kipp in my mind.

We drew within sight of the encampment, and I was beginning to worry as Kipp had not signaled me for the last hour. Suddenly, he came into view, running hard, his tongue hanging from effort. I was torn between wanting to chastise him for causing me such worry and grabbing him and hugging his neck. I chose the latter.

"Sorry," he said, "I was running so fast to catch up that I had to use all my energy for that; I didn't mean to excite you."

Perdy's voice broke into our reunion.

"Your beast is back. Now into the stockade with both of you. No time to tarry."

The other settlers who had gone to the river met our small group with stressful news: someone or something had disturbed their traps and nets and there was no bounty to be had that day. They spent their time trying to repair what they could, with the grim reality that whatever had done the damage could easily return, and they could not spare a man to guard the area. Charles, one of the men who had returned, was beside himself and finally gave voice to their collective beliefs and fears.

"John," he began, addressing Waite, "we have to face up to the fact that we cannot survive here any longer." His thin face was ashen, his long hair hanging in wispy lengths about his shoulders. "No matter what we do, that thing out there," he motioned to the forest, "seems to read our minds and counter us. The devil wants our very souls, I tell you, and I will no longer sit still and wait for him to take mine."

Waite grabbed his arm, thinking that he had to gain control of the sentiment of the people lest they split apart. He was correct in that they had a better chance at survival as a group versus splintering their numbers.

"Charles, take hold and calm yourself. We cannot be divided at this time. You know it takes all of our efforts to survive."

Charles stared at him, his thoughts betraying his inner conflict; he was not confident enough to pursue his challenge of Waite's authority, but his fear was intense and ever present. Waite, sensing his hesitation, spoke up.

"Let us unload the barrels of water we have brought from the river. We repaired the traps, so we will return in the morning and see if goodness has favored our efforts." After a pause, he added, "Charles, I need your help."

The two men stared at one another before a subtle drop of Charles's shoulders indicated his submission to Waite's leadership. Noting this, Waite clapped the younger man on the back. With that he walked toward the cart that was used to transport water. I wondered, for a moment, why they had built the settlement such a distance from the river but decided it was prudent since this was basically a coastal plain, probably subject to floods. The encampment was actually built on a rise and it would have taken massive flooding to endanger the home sites. All I know is that water was at a premium. The question of water came to mind as Perdy and I returned to her cabin.

"Perdy," I asked, "with water so valuable, how is it you conduct your washing and bathing?" My queries were not just anthropologic curiosity; I was getting a whiff of distinct body odor from myself, as well as everyone else.

"Having been on a ship, you certainly are accustomed to shortages of fresh water, are you not?" Without waiting for my answer, she said, "We take clothes to the river to wash. During warmer weather, we bathe there, too. And the men built a small structure in which we can heat water and bathe in the cooler months." Her thoughts trailed off and were simple to read as she added mentally, 'when it is safe'. She then resumed her conversation with me adding, "And sometimes, we bring water to our homes and bathe as best we can here." She disappeared for a moment to her bedroom and returned with a small stack of clothes. "Here, these belonged to my sister Ella, who was much your constitution. I know you will need a change as yours become soiled." So, I did stink and appreciated her tactful way of approaching the subject.

"I think I will take Kipp tomorrow and go to the river for a bath, if you don't mind."

"I really think no one should go anywhere without a weapon, but your beast is large and probably could protect you if needed. Anyway, the men will be returning there, so you can go with them." She excused herself to go outside for a moment. I took the opportunity to ask Kipp why he had not commented on my body odor.

"I think you smell nice, and now I don't have any trouble finding you in a crowd."

"Very funny, Kipp," I replied sarcastically.

Later that night, Kipp and I had fallen into a deep sleep; the day's activities had exhausted me more than I expected. I was suddenly awakened by a frantic Kipp, who had left our pallet on the floor and was scrambling at the door to the cabin, scratching with his feet hard enough to score the dense wood.

"Petra, hurry! Open the door!"

"What is it?" I asked, struggling to my feet, my back stiff from hours of gathering nuts.

"Hurry, something terrible is happening. Let me go!"

I pulled the door back, and Kipp almost knocked me down as he rushed past. Grabbing a shawl, I raced after him; Perdy had been awakened, and without a question, she darted after us. It was dark, quiet, the small village illuminated by a full moon that hung overhead. The night was so clear that every star was visualized, dotting the sky with familiar constellations.

Kipp ran to the stockade guard tower that was the furthest from our cabin. Placing his forepaws on the ladder, he began to bark frantically and was literally trying to crawl up the ladder, only to fall back to the ground.

"Kipp, what is it?" I asked.

"The man up there ..." he replied. "Something terrible has happened. His life force is gone; I was too late." John Waite and several of the other men, awakened by Kipp's persistent barking, ran up behind us.

"What is the meaning of this disturbance?" Waite began. "Can you make your beast stop that infernal noise?"

He took a step forward, aiming a kick at Kipp, who nimbly avoided the cuff. At that point, it occurred to Waite that his man in the guard tower was suspiciously quiet during the melee.

"Matthew! Is all well with you?"

There was no answer. I knew already, from the lack of mental presence, that Matthew was dead. And there was something else I had never experienced—there was an aura, an afterglow, of Matthew's thoughts and feelings right before he died. He had seen something which was unbelievable and horrible. The experience was so intense that it lingered in the atmosphere like wisps of smoke from a smoldering fire.

Waite looked at the other men, and swallowing hard, he began a slow ascent of the ladder. When he gained the top and peered over the side, all of us saw him suddenly stiffen, and it might have been my imagination, but it looked as if his knees almost buckled. His thoughts were filled with horror, and I did not have to see the body to know what had happened—Matthew's head had been crushed, and the small guard post was spattered with blood and tissue. Without looking down, Waite asked one of the men to bring a blanket.

"What has happened, John?" Perdy called out.

"Matthew is dead," he answered.

"You mean Matthew has been murdered," Charles said.

At that point, the remainder of the settlers joined us, the commotion having awakened all. Kipp nuzzled my hand and drew my attention to a young woman who had pushed her way through the small gathering. It was the gentle Alice, Matthew's wife. Without a word, she collapsed and was caught by several of the others. Perdy took the lead.

"Bring her to my cabin; I will see to her."

I lingered behind a moment, watching the men who made preparations to recover the body. Per John Waite, they would double the guard and all were in agreement. As Perdy was walking towards her cabin with the small group who were assisting Alice, Waite gazed after her and I picked up on a distinct whiff of guilt, coming from him. What could that be about, I mused. He glanced at me and caught me staring at him. His thoughts, for a flash, were distinct: 'Did she tell you?' he wondered. It all came together at that moment, even if I could not verify the facts, but I had learned to trust my instinct and intuition. Waite had some sort of illicit liaison with Nell, Perdy's sister, either by force or coercion; I would have guessed force was involved, given the nature of his hidden thoughts. Perdy knew of this, and thus her hatred was nurtured and grew. I understood now why Perdy hovered over all the ladies in the camp, including me, as if she was a mother hen.

I broke the intensity of the moment by asking, "Shall I

leave my Kipp here while you are working? He is a very good watch dog and will sound the alarm if anything approaches the wall."

Several of the men nodded their thanks, and with a mental note to Kipp that he was to be careful and observe, I took my leave and went to the cabin where Perdy was seeing to the needs of the grieving Alice. I found them sitting on my thin mattress before the fire, Alice cradled in Perdy's arms. Silently, I dropped to the floor nearby, touched by the sight of Perdy's chapped and work worn hands smoothing the flaxen hair of the much younger woman. Alice's head had fallen forward, her golden tresses covering her tear stained face. Perdy was murmuring nonsensical phrases, much as one would in comforting a child.

After a while, Perdy looked up at me and said, "Stay with her, please, while I go draw some fresh water."

I quickly took her place and Alice limply drooped against my arm. Her mind was filled with churning thoughts, the main theme of which was one of extreme guilt and remorse. She gripped my arm for a moment and turned her reddened face towards me. Her eyes had that unfocused quality when one has turned inward in grief and pain. But her thoughts kept coming full circle again and again, and lodged within them were memories of what she considered to be a murder. Imbedded in her tortured mind were names, most of which were familiar to me....that is, until she thought of a man named Edward. Who was that, I wondered, having not met anyone by that name. I couldn't determine how the puzzle pieces fit, but Alice clearly connected these memories with the entity that had killed her husband. The wraith or spirit who wandered the woods had been summoned to wreak vengeance upon the colonists in retribution for the death of the unnamed person who haunted her mind. She was entirely too fragile for me to manipulate her into revealing more, so I would bide my time and wait for another moment, perhaps with Perdy or another one of the colonists.

Perdy returned, Kipp alongside, and used the cool water to bathe Alice's face. By this time, she had dropped back on the mattress. She was clinging to my arm, so I reclined next to her. Perdy seemed satisfied that I was competent to care for her, so she once again left the cabin, her intent to help the others secure the blockade. Kipp walked slowly to where Alice and I lay.

"Petra, I bear some guilt over all this. If I'd done a better job, I might have been able to get to her husband before he was killed."

"That's nonsense, Kipp!" I replied sharply. "The only one responsible is whoever or whatever is hiding in the woods right now." Softening my tone, I asked, "Could you pick up anything out there?"

"No. Whatever it was, it left quickly, and the death aura colored everything; that is all I could read."

Alice looked up for a moment, and Kipp and I stopped our silent exchange to attend to her. She reached her trembling hand out and curiously stroked Kipp's ruff.

"His fur is soft," she commented. "I had thought it would be harsh to touch, but it is not."

Kipp, perceiving her need for comfort, dropped down next to her and carefully placed his muzzle across her chest. She gave a soft sigh, and I knew that his presence helped her to feel safe. The small enclosure of the cabin combined with the crackling warmth of the fire encircled us in a cocoon of security. We stayed like that all night, with her dozing off from time to time, her small hand tangled in the mass of Kipp's fur. At some point, Perdy quietly returned and, with a glance at me, nodded in satisfaction. After that, she went to her room to gain some sleep before the sun made its early appearance.

CHAPTER 18

The subsequent days passed as we fell into an uneasy routine. Alice never returned to her cabin and stayed with us—Perdy, Kipp and me. She seemed to have fixated her energy on Kipp and obviously felt more secure and safe in his large presence. Waite had managed, for the present, to convince the others to remain at the encampment. His argument was sealed when a heavy, early frost fell on the night following Matthew's murder. It would be ill advised to try and move the colony in the midst of a premature winter. He had, however, agreed that they would look at moving further inland next spring.

I shared with Kipp some of my thoughts from the night of Matthew's murder. He was concerned over my impression that Waite might have committed some type of sexual assault on Perdy's sister and agreed, from his reading of the tenor of Waite's violent fantasies as well as his suppressed and controlled nature, that he needed to be watched—and carefully.

The men were doubling up to guard the village at night. Due to that, combined with the duties during the daylight hours, they were quickly becoming exhausted. There were simply not enough bodies to do all that had to be done for survival coupled with the need to constantly guard the encampment from attack. Consequently, several of the women were instructed in how to load and fire the weapons. Perdy, in particular, had an aptitude; it probably helped that she displayed little fear of most things.

After we finished our supper one night, Kipp, who had been lying comfortably within the range of the fire, rose with ease, but his thoughts were urgent.

"Petra, we need to go outside—now."

I tried to appear casual as I told the others that we were going outside for some air. This was a poor excuse, since it was uncomfortably cool beyond the confines of the snug cabin, but that was all I could manage. As I opened the door, Kipp darted past me, his large body brushing my legs. I trotted after him across the compound; he was headed toward the rear guard house, the one where Matthew had died.

"It's out there, Petra. Hungry, searching, it wants to spread terror again—tonight."

I confess, I had never wished for greater skills than I did so now. Focusing, I could discern something, a presence, moving towards us but was unable to really determine any clarity of thought or purpose. I stayed silent, so as not to disturb Kipp's concentration.

"As it comes closer, I can read more of its thoughts. Petra, I've never experienced anything like this. It's as if it is filled with many voices, many entities; there are multiple voices talking, as if the creature is torn between which direction to follow, which path to take." He paused before adding, "The thoughts seem to be patterns that are human, but it also thinks of itself as an animal. Whatever it is, it's full of rage and thinks it's being directed to kill others."

The entity must have been moving rapidly towards us, because I was starting to pick up waves of emotion and a chaotic flood of disorganized thoughts. I was torn between sounding the alarm and remaining quiet so that I could continue to read the maelstrom that had targeted our island of humanity. The decision was no longer mine when Charles, who was in the nearest guard tower, called out to me. Whatever was out in the woods stopped its progression at the sound of his voice, and I felt it slowly melt away. It would choose another time.

We returned to the cabin. Alice had drifted off to sleep in the small bedroom. Perdy was sitting before the fire, fabric piled in her lap, making repairs on some clothing. Kipp, wagging his tail, walked over and gave her an affectionate head butt to which she smiled and ruffled his fur. It was difficult to not like Perdy. This was my opportunity.

"Perdy, may I ask you a question?" At her tacit response, I continued. "Is there someone here named Edward whom I have not met?" She gave a visible start and paled.

"Who told you of Edward?"

"Alice, in the midst of her grief, made mention of his name." It was not quite the truth but not exactly a lie, either.

"And what did she say?" Perdy was clearly not going to reveal anything unless she was compelled to do so.

I hesitated, trying to appear uncomfortable, reluctant to be forced to reveal any more. It was difficult to link up what bits and pieces I knew in any sort of organized fashion. Sometimes it was best to float an idea and even if it was wrong, the denial would help to consolidate a factual base.

"She expressed remorse over his death. And, uh, she thinks the evil spirit that plagues this place is seeking retribution."

Perdy took a deep breath. She was distressed at being placed in the position of violating the silence of the community.

"Petra, there is history here, and it is something with which I would not have burdened you. But since you will eventually be exposed to it, I see no reason to not tell you more." Kipp settled in next to us, ready for a story.

"When we first established this colony, we were led by Sir Edward Mann, who as fate would have it, was a kinsman of Queen Elizabeth. He was decent and well intentioned but, in retrospect, was probably ill suited for the task he was given. His young wife accompanied him, and shortly after we had made landfall, she gave birth to their first child." She paused and gave a faint smile. "I have never known of any man who loved his family more than Edward. When the fever ravaged our camp, his wife and child both died. He became deranged from his grief and descended into madness." Perdy took a ragged breath, her memories obviously painful.

"Believing that God had ordained our destruction, he murdered three of our members before he could be stopped. We were supposed to be civilized people, so we did the only thing we could—we had a trial, and he, of course, was found guilty." Perdy paused again, her lips dry, her face had paled. "John Waite had assumed leadership at that point and he, along with the other men, felt we should follow laws established in England. What were we to do with a murderer?" She stood up and paced the small room, Kipp following her movements with his eyes. "Petra, I am ashamed to say we hanged the poor, mad creature."

I walked over to her and gripped her arm. There was extreme remorse in her; she was unable to forgive herself or the others for what they had done.

"I am sure you all thought you had few options, being so isolated, so far away from home."

"That does not excuse us. We took the life of a man who was grief stricken, who had lost his sanity." She stared at her worn hands. "Afterwards, it occurred to Waite and the others that the man they had executed was of royal linage. If the Queen were to make discovery of this, we would all be in serious jeopardy. So they took the body off and buried it at a concealed location in the forest. We all swore that we would never reveal what had happened. I have to ask you now to also make that promise."

"Perdy, I was taken in when my need was great. You,

in particular, have been kind to me. I only want to help
you and promise I will never do anything that would
bring danger to your door." We sat before the crackling
fire, silent for several moments. Kipp was prodding me
to query further about the threatening entity. I decided to
plow ahead.

"So you all believe that the creature that resides in yon
woods is evil, perhaps some demon that has been
resurrected to avenge the death of Edward Mann?"

"What else could it be?" she responded. "Shortly after
that devil killed the first of our colonists, the natives who
lived nearby abandoned their village and left this area.
They were obviously fearful and believed this was
nothing they could counter. Since then, one by one, that
thing has killed off eleven of our members; it has chased
off the larger animals that we might use for food as well
as destroying our traps and nets and burning down our
modest field of fledgling crops."

"We need to go to the grave of Edward Mann," Kipp
was thinking. "In order to understand this problem, we
need to start at the beginning. And that would be the
execution and burial of Mann. You must get her to show
us where he is buried."

I replied that was going to be difficult to get her to
agree; I would try an idea I had, but it could be risky.
Perdy and the settlers were driven by superstition and
thoughts that were not based on science. My idea could
seriously backfire. *Symbionts* were adept at crafting
speedy solutions on the fly, this being a skill developed
from years of being stuck in the midst of exceptionally
precarious situations. While we were an intellectual
species, it did not bode well to over think situations and
lose the rhythm of the moment; sometimes, spontaneity
worked best when applied with a modicum of caution.

"Perdy," I began carefully, "in the West Indies, the
natives have a ritual by which they purify the grave of
the dead; their intent is to release negative spirits." I
paused to read her thoughts, which immediately took a

downward swing. "Have you ever heard of this?" She met my idea with disapprobation.

"What you suggest is against the word of God and it would not be condoned. You must not say this to anyone else here. If they were to think you were conducting heathen rituals...." her voice drifted off.

"Of course, you are right, Perdy," I quickly backtracked. "My father was of the same notion, and I would not have said anything except for my concern for all of you. We will not speak of it again." But we would; I would make certain of it. After she went to bed, Kipp and I lay there, deep in conversation.

"Petra, do you think I should plant a thought in her that will encourage her to take us to the burial site?"

"I think we should give her a little time and see if she can get past her knee jerk reaction. I basically tossed her an idea that goes against her core beliefs. But the fear and stress is so great that she might override her beliefs and take a chance." We drifted off, exhausted.

The next day fell into the usual pattern. The colony divided itself by thirds; one group went into the woods to forage; another went to the river to collect water and fish; the last stayed at the stockade to protect the home front. Perdy was in the latter group today, since the others felt she needed to help minister to Alice, who drew solace from Perdy's quiet strength. Kipp and I stayed, too, and worked with food preparation, cutting wood and other critical chores.

Perdy and I were stacking some firewood when surprisingly she turned to me and quietly said, "I will take you there." There was no further discussion. I glanced quickly at Kipp but he mentally shrugged his shoulders to let me know that he had taken no action to persuade her.

Our trip to the forest was to take place several days later, as I waited patiently on Perdy to decide upon the correct venue. She chose a day when we, again, had been left at the stockade. She did not ask permission, but rather told one of the men in charge that we—she, Kipp and I—were going out into the forest to look for some kindling. She was armed and we had Kipp, so our safety was not of concern. Taking a small cart with us, we trudged off, she and I pulling the unwieldy, heavy wagon behind us. I should learn to keep my mouth shut, but endless and boundless curiosity is the hallmark for my species.

"What caused you to change your mind?"

Her back stiffened slightly as her head came up. She stopped pulling the wagon for a moment as she gazed directly at me. "I thought about all of it and realized that I trust you. After all, you have tried to help us and have worked side by side with no complaint. My belief is that your soul is good."

I was without words.

Kipp laughed, saying, "So, is it so hard for you to take a compliment?"

After about ten more minutes, we arrived at a small clearing. Perdy slowly walked to a spot and indicated a mild depression in the soil with her downward drifting hand.

"Here is where he is buried."

It was unmarked and would have gone unnoticed, the area now covered with fallen leaves and other debris. Kipp walked over and began sniffing the ground, trying to look like a dog and not a creature with superior intelligence to us all.

"Petra, there are no human remains here. But there is something else. You must think of a reason to dig up the grave."

Great, I thought. My mind's wheels began spinning, as we stood there in silence. Finally I walked over to the cart, where I had foresight to place a small axe and pick. Fetching the pick, I walked to the grave site. Perdy's eyes were huge as she stared at me.

"So are you going to dig up his body?" she asked. "Is that part of the ritual?"

I had almost forgotten about the promised ritual to rid us of evil spirits.

"Yes, I need to see the remains."

With that pronouncement, using the pick, I softened the soil. This was going to be some work. Fortunately for me, the grave was very shallow and I quickly found the first edge of the coffin's lid. Working along the edge, I pushed the dirt off the lid, using the edge of the pick, all the while wishing I had a shovel. Perdy seated herself nearby, her thoughts anxious and conflicted. I noted she was inattentive to the surrounding woods, so I reminded Kipp to use his radar and scan, worried that the toxic entity might surreptitiously creep up on our location. Finally, the lid was completely uncovered. I anticipated it would be difficult to remove, but, to my surprise, the lid was not nailed on.

"Perdy, would they not have secured this top?" I asked.

"Yes, I saw them affix it myself."

"Well, it is not secured now."

I hesitated for a moment, mentally bracing myself for whatever lay within. Kipp had moved to my side but was still swiveling his head from time to time, scanning the woods. There was nothing out there, at least for now. Using the pick edge, I gingerly pulled the lid up and pushed it aside. Kipp and I both peered inside. To my shock, there was no human body in the coffin. What rested there was the decaying, putrid body of an animal. Kipp gazed at it but a few moments before concluding it was a wolf.

"What is it?" Perdy called, fearful to look.

"It is not Edward Mann," I responded. "It looks to be an animal."

She jumped to her feet and rushed forward. As she gazed into the wooden box, her thoughts betrayed her progression to hysteria.

"This is not possible," she shrieked. "A body cannot change like this. I saw them put him in this grave with my own eyes." Looking at me, she exclaimed, "Only the

behavior of evil spirits can explain this!" Her head
dropped for a minute; her gaze focused back at the
remains for a moment and a myriad of emotions played
over her expressive face.

Meeting my eyes again, she began, hesitantly, "When I
was a girl, I overheard a discussion that still haunts me
to this day. A friend of our family had returned from a
journey which had taken him through the Carpathian
Mountains. He told of a legend he had heard there, of
people who were half animal and half human. Petra, do
you think....?" Her voice drifted off with confusion. I
grabbed her arm.

"Perdy, calm yourself. Did it not occur to you that
someone may have dug up his body and placed this dead
animal in his coffin? There can be natural explanations."

"But who would have done such a thing?" She was
struggling to hear me and wanted to believe what I was
saying. My explanation was definitely preferable to the
alternatives.

"Maybe it is our creature that lives in the woods."

Disbelief flooded her face.

"Are you suggested that the demon who has plagued
us is a man?"

"Why not?" I answered.

"But what use would a man have with the dead body
of Edward Mann?" she asked.

"I don't know, Perdy. But we could be dealing with a
human; maybe one of the natives who once lived here is
deranged? He may have witnessed the execution or
burial, and due to his crazed thoughts, he dug up the
body and replaced it with this animal." I knew I was
working against a rigid set of beliefs, but she was trying
to hear my words. She could not fight a wraith; she
could, however, fight a man. She sat back on her heels
and looked at me.

"You had no ritual in mind, did you?" One would think
she would be angry with me, but she was actually
relieved.

"No, Perdy, and I ask you to forgive me for misleading you. I wanted you to show me this grave. It seemed to me that all of your problems started with the death of Edward Mann. And I believed in order to solve your mystery, we needed to return to the crux of the puzzle." She stared at me for a moment.

"Do you not believe in evil? Do you not think there is a devil who can work to destroy our lives?"

I answered her soberly and as honestly as possible.

"Perdy, I believe in good and evil. My father was a believer, but he also believed in the reality of people and their choices. I don't think what plagues you is a spirit; I think it is a man, a disturbed man—perhaps an evil man—but human."

"Why would you think that perhaps this being is a native?" she asked, hope in her tone.

"Well, it is the only logical conclusion, unless you have a missing colonist for whom you cannot account. Let's suppose that one of the natives from the village that once lay to the northwest became ill, an illness of his mind, and was sent away from the others. This man may have witnessed the hanging or the burial, but he eventually unearthed the body and replaced it with the mutilated wolf. All of this, mind you, was done due to his madness. The other natives, who had a respect for the dead, were horrified and fearful that you colonists might find this desecration and blame them. That would explain why they left this area so suddenly."

Kipp, listening carefully, said to me, "That makes sense, Petra, that the errant being might be a native. We know the location of the colonists, while the native numbers would be unknown to us. It also falls in line with my difficulty in interpreting the thought patterns; the cultural divide would be great."

Suddenly, I felt exposed and even though we were armed, I wanted to return to the stockade and quickly. If there was a man out here stalking us, he was intelligent with a deadly purpose. I placed the lid back over the decaying wolf and covered the shallow grave with alacrity. Kipp returned to his attentive posture, watching the surrounding territory for any sign of the malevolent being. In a short time, we took up the cart which I managed to pull slowly, while Perdy threw in small sticks and pieces of kindling as fast as she could, so that our cover story would not be questioned. We finally arrived at the gate and were faced with an apoplectic John Waite, who, upon meeting us, began berating our intelligence, lack of judgment and just about everything else he could sputter out.

After a few minutes of this humiliating display, he finally topped it off by saying, "Perdy, I have always valued your membership in this community. But your mind has obviously been affected by the recent events, and you have shown that you are poorly equipped to fend off the subversive influence of a person who is obviously poorly bred and of questionable morals."

Well, I mused, suppressing a yawn, he had to be talking about me. Having experienced many insults over my life, I found his to be not one of the most memorable. Truly it was a minor league type of effort. Kipp interrupted my smug humor by reminding me that Waite was in control and influential with his peers.

I started to speak up against Waite, but Kipp gave me counsel. "Stop, and allow Perdy to handle this. Listen to her thoughts—she is begging you to remain silent."

Indeed, I did listen and Perdy was internally hoping I would keep my mouth shut and let her manage the situation. Even though it disturbed me to let someone else take the hit meant for me, I remained silent.

"John, I beg your forgiveness." she began. Of course, her thoughts were otherwise—rebellious, angry, and berating him internally for the utter fool and hypocrite she found him to be. "Petra did not ask to go into the forest. I decided to go look for wood, and she offered to accompany me, bringing her dog so that I would be safe. If anything, the fault lies with me." She looked down at her feet, trying to appear humble. "I will not do anything like this again and will counsel with you first."

Nonplussed, Waite had no choice but to accept her apology lest he look like a prig. She had adeptly outmaneuvered him. He glared at her for a moment, showing the crowd that had assembled that he was the dominant male in this pride. Kipp and I both found his train of thoughts manipulative and unpleasant as he calculated how to gain favor in the face of his peers. He did not disappoint us.

"Perdy, I accept your apology and recognize that you, as a widowed woman, lack the leadership of your husband. I have, perhaps, failed in filling the void and will speak up more, as a brother and friend, to help guide you." There were murmurs of approval from the crowd. Perdy, however, had a mind filled with such dark thoughts that I almost took a step back.

Kipp said to me, "Wow, she really completely hates him, doesn't she? It must take all of her self control to not beat him to a pulp."

Waite looked at me for a moment, and then his eyes unconsciously darted to Kipp, who sat at my feet and stared back at him, for the first time not acting the part of a gentle and submissive dog. With curiosity, I tracked both of their thoughts. Waite again was seized with his sexual conflict and was calculating if he could get me alone and then either convince me to have sex or force me—it did not matter to him the method, just the outcome.

Kipp was thinking, "Just try it, big man, and see what happens."

"Kipp, please stop staring at him. Remember your role here and don't make it personal."

"Okay. It is just hard for me to tolerate his violent thoughts towards you."

I reached down and touched his head in a mild caress of affection as well as to ground him.

"We are here on a job. Waite does not know me and I

don't know him. It is business."

Kipp, with supreme effort, stood and, tail wagging, stepped to Waite and acted gentle and submissive. John thumped his side with his hand while exclaiming to all what a good dog was Kipp. I knew he was doing this for crowd approval, to look like a nice guy; internally he viewed the ever present Kipp as an impediment to his fantasy of assaulting me at some point.

With that, the crowd broke up, everyone drifting off to engage in the endless series of tasks and chores needed for survival. The group that had gone to the river actually returned with some fish; there would be fresh food tonight and everyone's attitude brightened just a bit. We were fortunate in that it was Mary's turn to prepare the kettle of food for the group, since she was the best cook of all, creatively using our stores of nuts, herbs and roots to create a truly succulent stew. As a bonus, she had even thrown in some dried, ripe persimmons that were harvested during late summer. The sweet taste was rare and welcomed.

Perdy took our pot to gather our portion of stew, bringing it back to the cabin as I worked to stoke the fire. We gathered as a little family—Perdy, Alice, Kipp and I—saying thanks for our meager meal. Even though Kipp was managing to obtain some food from foraging for small game, each of us would place a spoonful of our stew on a plate for him. He did not require it, but Perdy and Alice had learned to love him and wished to share; so he ate it, feeling their pleasure in the act of kindness.

Afterwards, we sat around the fire while Perdy mended clothes for some of the other colonists. I was pretty useless at that but actually knew how to weave baskets, having taken classes before in an evening session offered at Duke University. So I busied myself with a pile of dried rushes and began work on a new gathering basket. Alice, depressed and physically weak from her mental distress, was not asked to engage in any work, and she lay on the mattress, her arms around Kipp.

He nestled close to her and I noted her fearful mind notched down a bit. She was silent, but a few tears escaped from her eyes to roll down her cheeks. Kipp, ever the gentleman, gently licked them from her face. We would not have many more nights such as this one, where we were at peace.

CHAPTER 19

I was becoming increasingly concerned over the state of Alice's mind. Although to all observers she was passive, in actuality her thoughts were racing, filled with despair, self loathing and fleeing suicidal ideas. I knew almost nothing about mental health but could recognize depression when it was present in this obvious a fashion. Kipp was alarmed, having never experienced this sort of pain in a human. Since he had become attached to Alice, he thus bemoaned his inability to help her heal. I hesitated to mention any of my thoughts to Perdy, since I was certain suicide was an extreme taboo in this culture. She had absorbed a lot of my oddities, but I really did not need to push the issue right now. It was sufficient that Kipp and I would both watch out for Alice.

All of us, human and *symbiont* alike, were relieved that the murderer had not struck again and I hoped he had left the area. The colonists were taking nothing for granted, however, and continued their doubled efforts at security. The front entrance was closely guarded and no one could enter or exit without being seen. So it became one of those inexplicable events when one of our members went missing, and no one had seen her leave.

It began shortly before dusk, while I was filling our water bucket and gathering firewood for the evening, which promised to be cold. Perdy had been working on various projects all day, and I had interwoven helping her with making excuses to wander back and forth to the cabin to check on Alice. Kipp had taken on the responsibility of keeping constant watch on her. I blame myself for not recognizing that Kipp had quietly exhausted himself with keeping guard on us all, night and day. It was not his fault that he dozed off in the warmth of the cabin and thus did not see Alice silently rise and exit the dwelling. When I returned and bumped the door open with my bucket, Kipp awoke with a start.

"Hey, lazy bones, did you get a good rest?" I joked, glad he had napped. Kipp laughed in his good natured way and stood to stretch, shake and give a wide mouth yawn.

"What have you been doing?" he asked, ignoring the obvious, as I stood there with the bucket of water.

"Toting and fetching, my lad." Suddenly he looked at me and we had the same thought simultaneously.

"Where is Alice?"

With that, we both darted out into the courtyard. I ran from dwelling to dwelling to see if perhaps she was with another colonist. Kipp, his nose to the ground, tried to pick up her trail but it was difficult since there was so much cross over traffic. He even tried to pick up her distinctive pattern of thoughts, but that was not useful, either. Feeling progressively more worried, I began to shout her name. This, of course, drew the immediate attention of the few who were within the stockade. It was but a short time before Perdy rushed up, having been occupied with aiding the sick.

"What has happened?" she asked, exhaustion clearly playing across her mobile features.

"We cannot find Alice," I responded, the excitement clear in my voice. It was at that moment I recognized that even though I had not told Perdy of my private fears about Alice's mental instability, she had drawn the same conclusion as had I. In a second she directed the people who had drawn close to search the compound for Alice. As I continued my search, Kipp returned to my side.

"Petra, I can't find her here—either her scent or her life essence."

With that, Kipp dashed impulsively past the blockade entrance and, once clear of the settlement, put his nose to the ground again, trying to pick up her trail. I ran to the cabin to grab my coat, and by the time I returned, I could see him in the distance, his pose one of excitement.

"I found it!" he said, with a grunt of satisfaction. With that he took off at a slow lope, his head to the ground.

Shrugging into my coat, I mentally shouted, "Kipp, wait!" But he was gone. I started to run after him but was deterred at the entrance by one of the men who was determined to not let me go alone into the darkening forest. Surprising him, I grabbed his hand and bent his thumb back so that he released my arm. Free, I ran in the general direction Kipp had taken, trying to focus on his energy and thoughts so that I could find him. To my surprise, Perdy was right behind me, a kindling axe in her hand. I shot her a grateful glance, and we continued to hurry along, the brush dense, grabbing at our skirts as we tried to find our way in the rapidly falling darkness. After a short while, I paused, and we stood there, our breathing heavy as I focused my thoughts on Kipp.

"Where are you?" I silently called out to him. There was no answer, so we kept moving, but our pace slowed since we did not know in which direction to head. A few minutes later, I felt the familiar tingle in my mind—it was Kipp, close by. It is hard to explain but it is like the pinging of sonar; I would send out a thought, and he would send one back, and depending upon how the thought was received, I would recognize that I was drawing closer to him.

It was obviously more helpful when he finally called out to me, "We are at the graveyard. I have found Alice."

Feeling stupid for not having thought of that earlier, I said to Perdy, "Let's try the graveyard. She may have gone where Matthew is buried." She agreed and we turned our direction and sped up our pace.

It was dark now, but thankfully there was a full moon rising, or else we would have been in trouble. One can't imagine how dark the forest can be with absolutely no ambient light. After about a quarter mile hike, we came upon the area that the colonists had chosen for burials. The piece of land had been neatly cleared and a rough split rail fence marked the margins. The moon shone down like a spotlight and framed in the halo we saw Alice, crumpled on the ground, Kipp nearby. As we rushed up, I mentally let Kipp know how I felt.

"Don't you ever run off like that again! I mean it, Kipp." I wanted to cry but kept the tears at bay, not knowing if I was angry, frightened, or both.

"I'm sorry, Petra. I just felt it was my responsibility to find her, since her safety was entrusted to me." He paused before adding, "I didn't mean to scare you."

Perdy dropped down next to Alice and placed her hands on her shoulders. "Come now, dear, it is time we go home."

Alice turned her face towards us; her eyes seemed lifeless in the silver lit graveyard. Her tear streaked face was filthy from her having lain in the dirt. When she made no move to stand, Perdy nodded her head at me, indicating I should help her. With us on either side, we gently took Alice's arms and compelled her to stand. Her legs were wobbly and we supported her as her knees almost buckled. As I glanced at Kipp, something happened that was the most terrifying moment in my life. His body stiffened and, with extreme slowness, his head turned to stare past us into the dense woods; his hair began to rise along his spine and his whole posture became rigid. His mind became filled with fear, not for himself, but for us. It was but a moment later I discerned the source as familiar tangled thoughts entered my mind: our nemesis had returned and was rapidly approaching. Perdy glanced at my pale face and then at Kipp—her intuitiveness served her well.

"Alice, we need to go now," she said urgently. When Alice did not respond, Perdy gave her a sharp slap across her face. "Alice, now!" The slap seemed to waken Alice from her depressive slumber and she began to stumble along, with us on either side, prodding, supporting, and pushing her.

"Kipp, come!" I called out as he took up a defensive position behind us. The malevolent thoughts of our hidden pursuer became clearer to me, indicating he was drawing close. Oh, yes, he intended to kill us all if he could.

We exited the graveyard and were trying to run but found ourselves held back by Alice who was stumbling and staggering. Perdy kept up her encouraging words, holding Alice's arm with one hand and her axe with the other. I was on the other side, trying to keep moving while also watching out for Kipp, who was about ten yards behind us. He would run a few feet and then whirl to face the unseen one, crouching to bark savagely in an attempt to deter him. It was not working, however, and after a few moments, Kipp would turn and draw closer to us again, before making his defensive display in the face of our enemy. This was not going well, and based upon the increasing intensity of his thoughts, I knew he would reach us before we could get to the stockade.

"Perdy, give me your axe," I demanded. She started to refuse but we had no time to argue. I took it from her hand and pushed her shoulder hard. "Go, keep going, get back home and send help." With that I retreated a few steps to join Kipp, who once again was engaged in frenzied barking, his ruff coated with foam. Calling out into the dark, I cried, "If you come any closer, I will defend myself!"

I could read momentary uncertainty in his mind and then something else: he really did not want me—he wanted to get to Perdy and Alice. We could not hear his forward progression through the brush for a moment, before Kipp realized he had begun a slow circle around us. We adjusted our position, to once again place ourselves between him and the fleeing women. I could feel his rage at being thus thwarted, but he still did not want us. His thoughts were swirling, and the divergent voices within gave him a moment of uncertainty. But then we heard him began to rush forward, having apparently decided to rid himself of the annoying beings who stood between him and his prey.

"Kipp, run!" I shouted. The two of us turned as a unit and begin to flee towards the stockade. "Don't stop," I cried, breathlessly. We could hear the pursuer's heavy tread as he no longer worried about a stealthy approach. He was running, as were we. I stumbled once, catching my toe on a root but caught myself and redoubled my speed. It was then that we saw some lights in the near distance—a search party with lanterns was just ahead!

"Here, here we are!" I shouted. In a short time, a group of armed men led by John Waite had arrived and surrounded us. "He is back there," I gasped, breathless, pointing in the general direction. They all looked at one another with uncertainty, not wanting to confront whatever lay in wait. I did not blame them. Finally, however, Waite showed courage and summoning three others, they walked slowly into the forest in the general direction I had indicated. They moved as a tightly bunched group.

I dropped to my knees, trying to get my breath back. Even though I was in good shape, the combination of the physical exertion with the fear had severely winded me. Kipp drew close and frantically licked my face.

Charles remarked, "It is a good thing you had your beast with you, Mistress Petra. There is evil afoot tonight, and I doubt your axe could have found its mark in the heart of the devil." Glancing up at him, I staggered to my feet.

"That might be true, Master Charles, but I planned to give him a run for his money." Whoops! The modern day expression had leaked out of my addled mind, undisciplined due to fatigue, but for whatever reason,

Charles was amused and gave a soft laugh.

"You are not without courage, Mistress. But unless you plan to chase with your axe whatever demon lies thus, we need to return to the encampment." With that, he and another man took positions on either side of Kipp and me and accompanied us back home.

When we arrived, the colonists surrounded us, amazed that we had survived and grateful for what Kipp and I had done to save Alice. As they gathered to congratulate us, the remainder of the search party returned. John Waite looked at me with his pale eyes.

"It seems you have a heroic nature, Mistress Petra. You have returned our gentle Alice back to our embrace." He was saying nice things in front of the others, who were nodding their heads, but privately he was fuming. It irritated him that any woman could show strength and courage. He preferred the passive, wimpy variety.

"Well," I began, "the true heroes were Perdy and Kipp. I just ran along with them."

"But that is not true, Petra," Perdy's voice called out, as she stepped forward from behind the others. "I think that any of you who have had reserves about Petra's quality can now be reassured. She exposed herself to danger and death to help our Alice. She is fully a member of our society and certainly deserves our respect." She walked to where I stood with Kipp at my side.

"And for this one," she said, indicating Kipp, "he is as valuable as a guardian angel. Never have I seen such a wonderful beast. He seems to know what I am thinking before I know it myself."

Kipp looked at me and slowly closed one eye. He appreciated the humor of the moment.

CHAPTER 20

I am not certain, in a closed community of people who have absolutely no exposure to other humans, how certain diseases establish a tenacious foothold and flourish. But they can and they do. It was our misfortune that these people, who had been devastated by what sounded like typhoid fever, were now assaulted by some other illness that raced through our small group. The hallmark was intractable vomiting and subsequent diarrhea, which left the individual unable to take any food or fluids and so weakened as to not be able to stand.

It seemed to me that I had never seen such a small cluster of humanity suffer more misfortune in such a short interval of time. The one in the group who possessed the knowledge and skill in the use of herbs to manage illness had died in the first wave of typhoid that killed more than half of the colony. Perdy became the one to fill this void, basically by default. She had spent the most time with the former healer and knew a few of her potions. I tried to assist as best I could. It was a source of private embarrassment that I knew so little about herbal medicines despite my numerous travels into the past; I would change that in the future, I promised myself.

"Hand me that jar of dried Lion's Tooth," she ordered. "I shall make a mild tea and add a small amount of honey. Sometimes that can help to sooth the insides which are in turmoil." She added that when she next left the compound, she would look for a red elm.

"I was told that its inner bark can be dried and powdered and used to make a healing tincture."

I was dealing with people who did not know about germs, microbes or disease. But they did have presence of mind for John Waite to order that the afflicted be quarantined in three cabins on the far side of the encampment. He knew, as did the others, that history dictated if one became sick, all could become sick. If everyone acquired this particular illness, there would be no one able to gather food. So despite scientific knowledge, Waite just used basic good logic. For all his character flaws, he did have occasionally sound leadership skills.

The number of people left to find food, bring water and firewood was dwindling rapidly. We were forced to leave the camp with smaller numbers and the fear factor multiplied now, since people felt more vulnerable to our hidden adversary, who fortunately had not made his presence known since the terrifying night in the graveyard. If mine and Kipp's speculation was correct, maybe he was, indeed, a native and he had left the vicinity. Or, perhaps he had died of an unknown cause.

I awoke to a much colder morning than previously and was grateful for the heavy and familiar warmth of Kipp. Perdy and Alice were still asleep, so I took the opportunity to go draw a bucket of water from the community stock. The cold air had left a thin crust of ice on the water's surface—this I had to chip away in order to obtain what I needed.

Kipp accompanied me, and as I glanced at him, it occurred to me that his robust constitution had left him in a superior physical condition to the humans as well as to me. My metabolism was working to my advantage, but the slow and insidious deprivation was having a minor toll. This was not unusual and was one reason I worked to recover my constitution before this journey. Kipp shook himself hard, his auburn coat bristling in the cool air—vital and strong was he. The lupine members of our species were typically more vigorous than the humanoids, but even Tula could not compare with Kipp. His years in isolation had led to superb conditioning. There is something to be said for hard work in one's younger years. Abraham Lincoln was said to be a very strong and powerful older man, probably at least half due to chopping and carrying lots of wood as a young fellow.

"Petra, what do you think has happened to the man-beast of the forest?" Kipp had obviously coined his own phrase to describe our confusing watcher in the woods.

"I don't know; he could have moved on or died. I would imagine he's having as much difficulty as are we in procuring food. He is, after all, human and vulnerable. He may think he's a wolf, but he is not." Hefting the heavy water laden bucket, I noted the approach of John Waite who was carrying an armful of wood.

"Mistress Petra, a word, please."

I started to keep walking but reminded myself that my job was to investigate this colony and its path in time. Setting the heavy bucket down, I waited for his approach.

"I wanted to apologize," he began, "for my harsh words the other day." He smiled, but I recognized he was just attempting to manipulate me. "The stress has been great and I fear I overreacted. The burden of leadership has been much."

With difficulty, I kept the sneer from my face.

"Your apology is accepted, Master Waite. I need to get this water back to Perdy and Alice." He tried to insist that he would help me, but I picked it up and moved off as rapidly as I could short of actually running, leaving him staring after me, dark thoughts flooding his mind.

After a light meal, the four from our cabin met up in the community hall for assignments. There were so few able bodies at this point that strategic planning was a must. I volunteered to go into the forest and collect nuts. The others were immediately alarmed, their fear of our adversary pushing their response.

"You forget, my friends, I have my Kipp and with him at my side, I fear naught."

Actually, Kipp and I needed more time away from our companions, since their thoughts impeded our abilities to seek out and better understand the solitary and hidden human—if he, indeed, was still in the vicinity.

Perdy and Alice were to accompany a group to the river. Waite was taking four men into the forest to collect firewood. Their work would be difficult as they had to fell trees, saw them and split the pieces for firewood. The remaining would stay at camp, guard the four posts, care for the sick and work on food preparation. There were fish hanging in the smoke house that were being dried for storage to help sustain the colonists throughout the winter; these had to be removed and room made for more fish, if any were to be had.

I rushed back to the cabin to fetch a fabric bag I had constructed that hung cross body style to help me collect nuts as well as anything else edible. Alice kept touching my arm, her excessive anxiety oppressive and disturbing to my psyche. Perdy purposely distracted her so that Kipp and I could ease off. With that, we were gone, quickly making our way past the gate; within seconds we had vanished into the vast forest.

"Kipp, this is the first time we have been free of human thoughts and feelings since our arrival. And I, for one, welcome it."

"What would you have me do?" he asked.

"Well, I do have to gather nuts; so as I do so, I want you to work a large circle of coverage, starting at my location—sort of like a reverse spiral. Canvass as best you can and keep your mind open. See if you can pick up on his energy. If you get a hit, then we will decide what to do at that point."

One of the colonists had suggested a rough location for me to find nuts, this one having not been worked as aggressively as some of the others. With rapid steps, we finally located the general area, and as I began to work, Kipp likewise began his job. I would look up from time to time and see his burnished body weaving in an out of the brush. So far, nothing had occurred on his end, or mine for that matter. The air was still cool, but I noted a change in the wind. What had been a mild breeze was picking up significantly, and skyward, the cloudless blue was darkening with scudding clouds littering the horizon. There would be a storm later today, but not for a while, I calculated.

We continued thus for another two hours when our peace was disrupted by one of the colonists, a man named Simon, who had been sent to find us.

"Mistress Petra," he began breathlessly, "I have looked all over to locate you. "Mistress Perdy sent me. It seems that our Alice has lost her good senses. Overcome with her grief, she tried to throw herself in the river. When prevented from this, she began shaking and screaming, inconsolable in her attitude. She fears for you and your beast, Kipp. Mistress Perdy did all she could but to no avail. You are asked to come now to help with Alice." He paused, and I saw his eyes widen as he looked around the increasingly gloomy forest. Unconsciously, his hand gripped his rifle harder; his mounting fear was oppressive to me. Kipp, hearing his approach, bounded back and waited for my decision.

"Master Simon, I have only collected half of the nuts I had intended. You will take Kipp with you, as Alice is attached to him, and he will bring her comfort. I will finish what I am doing and meet all of you back at the stockade in a short time."

Kipp immediately nixed my idea, not willing to leave me.

"There's a crazy man running around out here killing people, and you want to stand here, unarmed. What's your plan? Will you throw a walnut at him if he approaches?"

"Kipp, you've done a thorough survey with no results. I'm not as skilled as you, but if he approaches, I'll know it and can retreat back to camp. Alice needs you and I can watch out for myself."

"I do not think I should leave you here alone with no guard," Simon remarked, speaking up to interrupt our telepathic dialog.

"But it is not your decision to make, Master Simon. It is mine. Call Kipp and he will go with you."

Reluctantly, for both Kipp and Simon, they walked off together in the direction of the river. Kipp, several times, looked over his shoulder at me. A couple of times he considered disobeying my directions and returning to my side but then would talk himself out of it in deference to my experience.

"It's okay," I kept telling him. "I will be fine and promise to be careful. Take care of Alice."

The sky overhead was gradually growing more threatening; the wind was disturbing what few leaves had clung tenaciously to the skeletal tree limbs. I hastened my pace of work, wanting to help the colony with as much food as I could supply. All the time, I kept my mind uncluttered, open, seeking any energy that might be nearby. Having stooped to pick up a black walnut, my hair tumbled into my eyes. As I stood slowly, stretching out my back and pushing my hair off my face, I felt a slight tickle, as if someone was nearby, perhaps watching me. Trying to look casual, I did a visual sweep but saw nothing.

In a moment, I felt the sensation again. There was a human mind, just coming into my range. Kipp, with his exceptional talents, would have picked up on this energy with alacrity, while I managed to slowly plod along. Taking a seat on a fallen tree trunk, I completed a full minute of deep breathing and blocked out all other external distractions. Yes, it was there, nearby, but not so close as to be a physical threat to me.

"Who are you?" I wondered with curiosity. His mind was difficult to follow. There were aspects of his thinking that was like a feral animal, stalking me, hunting a human for the kill. But just as quickly, he would regard me tenderly, thinking that he needed to help me gather food for the winter. As I continued to focus, I perceived the distinct voice within his head, a voice that would command him to violence. This pattern of chaotic thoughts was what had confused Kipp. But I knew what it was—this man was psychotic, and the divergent voices were hallucinations. As he heard the voices, so I could hear them in his mind. Following his thoughts was like pursuing a banking pinball as it careened about inside the noisy machine that was his brain.

He was creeping closer and as he did, the tenor of his thoughts began to change. 'You are not one of them; you have not been condemned to death yet. You best take care, little sister, lest they kill you, too.'

So, he distinguished me from the colonists and his nihilistic thoughts diminished. But he was still insane, his mind filled with paranoid and conflicted ideas. He did seem incredibly fearful and grossly mentally ill to my unpracticed eye. I was a historian and my knowledge of mental illness was just slightly greater than my knowledge of herbal medicines. I slowly rose and turned my body, facing his direction. After a few more minutes of slow progression, his form came dimly into view— still at a distance. One looks back and questions stupid actions, and I had cause, later, to wonder if I had completely gone mad, too. There I stood, unarmed, alone in the forest, facing this killer whose mind was shredded by madness, as he slowly advanced on me. But I had to know and was unwilling to turn away.

The wind continued to pick up, rattling the leaves and underbrush, the sounds contributing to the eeriness of the moment. I can only attribute that, along with my extreme focus on the man in the woods, to cause me not to hear or perceive the approach of John Waite. He was within a few feet of me when it hit me and I whirled, startled. Odd, he frightened me more than the killer in the forest.

"Mistress Petra," he began, "I came to see if you needed help."

"No, thank you. I was just starting back." I tried to walk past him when he grabbed my arm.

"Why do you hasten so?" he asked.

Any amateur *symbiont* could have read his thoughts, which were revolting. He meant to coerce me into having sex or to force me. And he had already problem solved the forced part—if that happened, he would kill me so that I could not tell anyone and make it look as if the unnamed killer had done the act. The rage and resentment he had harbored towards me had finally smoldered to this flash point. I was in serious trouble.

"Master Waite, let go of my arm." I decided to take an assertive position and see if he would release me. He was, after all, a man who lacked confidence.

"I have been thinking of you," he said, still gripping my arm. "I know you think of me, too. I can tell by how you gaze at me."

At that point, I pulled my arm loose and began to walk past him. Well, he showed himself to be a man of impulse, and impulsivity is the one characteristic that *symbionts* are not well equipped to handle. Reaching out with his fist, he punched my jaw, hard. Dazed, I fell to the cold ground, berating myself for having been so naïve. As I hit the ground, all of my self defense training flew out of my head. He had managed to hit just the correct spot to as incapacitate me for a moment. A nasty opportunist, he followed me down to the ground, covering my body with his. I got my senses back enough to begin to struggle in earnest and all I received for my trouble was another cuff to the side of my head. As he began to pull at my clothes, I had a moment of intense awareness; the thoughts of the man who had been hiding in the woods had intensified and were filled with rage and thoughts of death. None of this was good, I thought.

As I was in the midst of working up a defensive move against Waite, there was a rushing sound of footsteps in the fallen leaves. Waite looked up, screamed, and then his head simply disintegrated, blood, bone and tissue splattering on my face and body. What remained of his body was roughly pulled off me. I looked up to see a tall man, his face blackened with dirt and filth, garments tattered, a combination of native and colonial discards; he wore a wolf's pelt with the head sandwiched against his, the remainder of the fur flowing down his back as would a cape.

"To your feet, little sister; we must flee lest they find us and kill us." His voice was not native; he was English. Reaching his hand down, he grasped mine and pulled me swiftly to my feet. Everything coalesced at that moment as all the elements of the universe aligned.

"I am grateful for your assistance, Sir Edward. I am called Petra."

"I know you, little sister; you have the beast which guards you. You are not one of the condemned ones." He swiveled his head for a moment, scanning the woods. "Come, we must go now."

I stood there, trying to steady my balance, still shaking my head a little to clear my mind.

"I am grateful that you protected me, but I need to go back to the colony."

That was obviously the wrong thing to have said. His eyes widened, his countenance darkened. His thoughts, which had been relatively clear, started to accelerate with the divergent ideas laced with paranoia. I noted his hand strengthening its grip on the large club he had used to kill Waite, as he struggled internally with what he wanted to do and what the voices were telling him to do. We stood there, staring at each other. And then I felt Kipp, reaching out to me, running as fast as possible to my location.

"I'm coming, Petra," he called out to me.

"Kipp, stay clear. Let me handle this."

He didn't answer and turned me off as one would turn off the volume of a radio. But I could feel his approach. He was filled with primal energy and his focus was to get to me; Kipp was an unstoppable force—now.

Sir Edward, having finally won his internal battle, decided to not harm me and began to retreat into the woods. Grabbing my arm in a firm grip, he began pulling me along behind him. I passively resisted, not desiring to go but not wanting to provoke more rage in him since I knew his mind was balanced as if on the edge of a knife. Overhead, the sky was beginning to rumble with thunder and the wind had intensified another notch.

I knew that Kipp was now about 100 yards out, his body low to the earth, his pace rapid. He was circling in from the southeast, his mind focused in pinpoint tunnel vision; his feet were racing silently through the dense bracken. I tried one more time to get him to stop to no avail. The Kipp I had known, a logical and reasoned being, had become purely primitive and reactive. At the last minute, he turned into us, and, as misfortune would have it, Edward turned his head with preternatural awareness in time to see Kipp launch his body in an attempt to knock him off his feet. Instinctively, Edward swung the club and it struck Kipp on his right shoulder. The force of the blow carried his body off into the bush.

Symbionts, for as ancient a species as are we, are always discovering something new. I almost collapsed to the ground as I experienced Kipp's physical pain when his shoulder and leg were shattered. I knew that he was still alive, though gravely injured. Thinking quickly, I commanded Kipp to be still. Sir Edward, who was still full of adrenalin, started towards him.

"Oh, please," I cried, grabbing at his arm, "let him be. He is my only friend, and you have injured him. You can see he cannot bring you any harm."

Placing my body between him and Kipp, I decided that

whatever happened, I would not let him go after Kipp. Maybe he could still listen to reason. We stood there for a long time as Edward struggled to get his rapid and excited breathing under control. Kipp did as I bade him and lay quietly without a whimper, but his pain was great and he needed medical attention quickly. To complicate matters, the storm that had threatened drew closer and thunder began to rumble overhead. Finally, Edward's shoulders dropped, and grabbing me by my wrist again, he began to pull me off into the forest. It was at that moment a familiar voice called out.

"Release her and leave this place—whatever you call yourself." It was Perdy, strong and confident, her fear ebbing as she took control of herself and the situation. As he turned to face her, his free hand—the one that carried the massive club with which he had taken so many lives—began to lift threateningly. Perdy shouldered the rifle she carried and without hesitation fired point blank. Edward staggered backwards for a few steps, clutching his chest, having dropped his hold on me. He fell back onto the leaf strewn ground, moaning for a moment before silence overtook him. I felt his life force slowly ebb.

I walked forward and gripped Perdy's arm in gratitude before moving on to Kipp's side. Perdy walked, almost in a daze, to the body of Edward. As she stared at his face, confusion and disbelief were rapidly followed by comprehension and grief; she had not recognized him, until now. She had killed the scourge of the camp, but in doing so, had taken the life of a man who had once been her friend. I knew her well enough to recognize she would never find ease with her choice which, as it happened to be, was the only one open to her. She saved my life and Kipp's.

I knelt by the silent Kipp. He moved his head weakly and tried to thump his tail at my approach. "Be still, you goof," I said. Gently examining him, it seemed the club had caught him directly on his right shoulder and upper leg, shattering the bones; from the area struck, I assumed some ribs were fractured, too. There was no way for me to know about internal injuries. I had to get Kipp home quickly.

Perdy had, after saying a silent prayer for Edward, walked over to the remains of John Waite; she had no words for his soul and merely stared coldly at his body. She did have a moment of concern for his wife, Mary. Then she rushed to my side, kneeling in the dead leaves where Kipp lay.

"Perdy! Kipp has been badly injured. If you can go back to the camp and get me a wagon, please, we will take him home." I regretted I had to lie to her, my friend and savior, but it was necessary to get her away from this location. Perdy gazed at Kipp and ran her hand softly along his flank.

"Yes, I will go for help." The minute she darted away, I refocused on Kipp.

"Listen to me; this is going to be very difficult, but we must travel home now, so that I can get you the medical help you must have. So, Kipp, despite your intense pain, you are going to have to find some way to focus with me."

He didn't reply; all of his thoughts were internalized on the pain, which was overwhelming. I ran my hand gently along his side and he turned his head, briefly, only to fall back weakly onto the cold ground.

This was not going to work, I thought. Something had to happen before Perdy returned. Wracking my brain, I tried to remember anything from my years of travel that might be of use in this situation. There was something there in the recesses of my mind, something ancient, a moment in time that I happened across while reading one of Fitzhugh's volumes one day when I had idle time on my hands. Taking a few deep breaths, I worked to center myself so that I could recover the memory. When one is uncertain, I told myself, it is the supreme situation in which one can make a choice, convince oneself to be confident and make it happen. This was that time—for me and especially for Kipp.

"Kipp, listen to me. I remember reading where a *symbiont* once used physical contact in conjunction with the mental connection to assist an injured companion. He was able to literally subdue the other's pain by taking on half of the burden, thus placing their bond back in balance." I could feel his skepticism. "No, really, I'm telling you the truth. I read about it in one of Fitzhugh's books."

"So what do we do?" he ground out.

"We'll start by deep breathing and meditation; this will be difficult for you, since you're having trouble with focus. But do the best you can. Once we get as relaxed as possible, I'll place my hands on your shoulder, and I want you to mentally release your pain into the palms of my hands. As your pain then lessens, we'll proceed with focusing on traveling back home."

"Petra," he began, but I cut him off.

"Kipp, for this to work, you must believe in what I'm telling you; you must trust me completely."

"You know that I do."

"Prove it then, and let's begin."

We both began deep abdominal breathing, Kipp wincing a little at the friction on his battered ribs. After a minute, I rubbed my hands together to warm the surfaces and then gently placed them on his shattered shoulder and the proximal area of his ribcage.

"Let it go, Kipp; let it flow out into my hands." I felt my palms tingle, and then there was a rush of warmth followed by excruciating pain. Instinct would have made me recoil, but I forced myself to continue the contact and mentally encouraged Kipp to keep releasing the energy. As he did so, I felt Kipp's mind clear somewhat; the lessening of pain was enabling him to begin to think of the steps for us to travel home.

"That's it. Good." I encouraged him, not wanting him to stop for fear of harming me. After a few minutes, I felt our bodies and mind were as balanced with one another as was possible, given the circumstances.

"Kipp, I want you to rid your mind of pain and worry—focus completely on home. Think of Lily, who is waiting for you to take her into the garden, where the dew off the grass collects on her paws; remember how she shakes her feet, trying to rid them of the damp? Think of our early mornings together, me with my coffee and you chasing Lily as she hunts for a spider." I paused and ran my hand along his fur. "Remember how we settle in at night, as I read a book and you rest next to me, your head on my chest? Think of all of it, and we will be home."

He did as I bade him as I, too, focused on home. Feeling the familiar sensations of travel, there was a sense of moving forward, my body and Kipp's stretching out, hair and fur flowing with the speed of it all. I couldn't stop to think of Perdy and the others; that would come later. Right now, all I could do was focus on the journey home. The vortex of time had opened its portal and into it we fell.

CHAPTER 21

In subsequent days, I was to think often of Perdy, Alice, Sir Edward and all of the colonists who had touched my life and thus changed me. Kipp's recovery proved to be a lengthy one, as he had to undergo multiple surgeries until his shoulder and leg were repaired. After that was physical therapy, an extensive process that involved water exercise so as to encourage range of motion and strengthening with no weight bearing. I rarely left his side and used our new found skill of pain sharing through physical touch to help him in recovery.

I prepared myself for the disapprobation of the Twelve, but to my surprise, they were encouraging and actually shouldered most of the blame for what had happened. Kipp and I, however, did not fault them or anyone else. The union of *symbionts* was to be compared to aging a fine wine—one can open the keg, take a taste, and decide that the mixture needs more time in order to reach the peak of perfection. *Symbionts* aged and grew together in such a manner. And it is only through error that we learn and have the opportunity to change and grow. Kipp, for all his amazing skills that were superior to any the rest of us might possess, was relatively young and untested; symbiosis was a new situation to which he had to adjust. So, he did what a juvenile lupine might do: he had reacted impulsively. His broken shoulder and leg were evidence of such, but they were also proof of his courage, loyalty and stout heart. Kipp was, and always would be, my companion for a lifetime.

When we arrived home, Tom Hughes was one of the first to meet us and, upon seeing the extent of Kipp's injuries, realized these were beyond his ability to heal. He arranged for orthopedic surgery at the veterinary school at NC State. That was, perhaps, the only instance in the following weeks, that I was not with Kipp. The vets at NC State viewed Kipp as a really big, nice looking dog; my obsessive need to be in constant contact would have seemed a bit too unusual, even for people accustomed to fanatical dog owners. Tom assumed the care after surgery and transported Kipp back to a ward at the institute. We placed a mattress on the floor, and Kipp and I lay there, his muzzle on my shoulder as I threaded my fingers lightly through his fur. His pain was significant, and I tried to share the burden when I could—and when he would allow. We used a harness to lift him so that he could drink, eat and relieve himself. Usually it was Tom and me or one of the technicians. Kipp chafed a bit at his helplessness but took it all in better grace than would I.

The Twelve decided to delay any true debriefing and limited questions to superficial ones. Juno came by frequently, along with Philo. And much to Kipp's delight, even old Fitzhugh dropped by, carrying the silly Lily in his arms. She hopped down and pranced on tip toes on the mattress, rubbing her sides against Kipp's muzzle before settling down between his forepaws.

"So how was she, Fitzhugh?" Kipp inquired.

"She got into my manuscript of the fall of Troy and managed to eat the corner off of one of the pages as well as knock a mug of tea over a page and ruin the script." His voice was harsh as he answered but his thoughts betrayed his tenderness. He was clearly in love with her. Kipp realized this, too, and subtly placed a thought in Lily's feline brain that she should go with Fitzhugh as he turned, reluctantly, to leave. Lily sprang up and chased him down the hallway, almost tripping him as she weaved about his feet. Audibly grumbling and complaining, he bent down to fetch her and placed her up on his shoulder for the ride back to the library.

"That was kind of you, Kipp. I realize you love her, too. But you're willing to give her up." Kipp was a better creature than most of us. He looked at me with his expressive amber eyes.

"She loves us all and thinks I am her mother. But even mothers know when it is time to cut the cord, and Fitzhugh needs her. Besides, every time we go on a journey, she will be left behind. She'll be better off with him."

"So", I asked, trying to sound casual, "are we going on another trip one day?"

"Of course," he answered, startled that I would have any doubt.

"There have been *symbionts* in the past who, after one travel, decided to never do it again." I paused for a moment. "There were some who thought I should quit after Tula was killed." Looking at Kipp, I decided it was time to say all the things I had been suppressing. "Kipp, when I saw that club swing at you, it was as if it was in slow motion. I mean, what if I'm not a good partner for this? First it was Tula and now it's you. Maybe I am the reckless one some seem to think I am." Kipp stared at me for a moment before giving a deep sigh.

"Petra, I was responsible for my injury, not you. I lost my focus and was impulsive. You were telling me to stay away, let you handle it, and I wasn't willing to listen."

"So, did you learn anything?" I asked. Kipp smiled internally at my query.

"I learned to duck next time." He regarded me for a moment before becoming serious. "Actually I did learn something. I didn't know until that moment how much I love you. And if I'd been killed due to my hasty behavior, then I wouldn't have been able to help you later. I think I learned that one can love and be deliberate in one's actions." I started to speak but he shushed me.

"No, I'm not finished yet. Love involves responsibility, and I think that's the biggest lesson for me. I've heard many humans speak of love, but their actions don't back up the statement. If I love you, I am compelled to act in ways that benefit you."

By this time, the tears were flowing freely down my face. *Symbionts* have an advantage to humans at times like this—Kipp knew my heart and didn't have to follow up his comments with inane and annoying questions such as, 'Did I say something wrong?'. Kipp had learned the lesson that caused humans to struggle for a lifetime, often without finding an answer: love, true love, is selfless. Yes, we were safe at home. Kipp would walk, eventually, and we would travel again, at some point in the future. All was right with the world.

THE SYMBIONT
TIME TRAVEL ADVENTURES
SERIES

*Turn the page for an
excerpt from*

TOMBSTONE,
1881

The Symbiont Time Travel
Adventures Series

Book Two

T.L.B. Wood

All that was visible from the window to my right side was the scene of unending bronze desert; the sun was tilting towards the west, and shadows were beginning to lengthen off into the distance. Shades of lavender and deep violet threaded their way through the blue sky, arching down to the far horizon. By now, Kipp and I had become accustomed to the gentle rocking of the stage; it was oddly hypnotic, and I jerked my head up when my chin abruptly dropped to my chest. I glanced at Kipp who reclined across from me, his large body occupying the entire bench seat.

"I'm glad we came," he commented. "It's interesting, and I'm enjoying the change in scenery."

I nodded my head; Kipp suddenly craned his neck, and his ears pricked upright. His superiority to me in terms of raw symbiont skills was such that he picked up on the thoughts of our drivers, Pete and Dave, before I did. From their dialog, it was apparent we were being followed by men on horseback. Because of the slowness of the team pulling the coach, it would only be a matter of minutes before the unnamed pursuers would apprehend us. Kipp turned his head slightly.

"They are bandits... highwaymen," Kipp commented.

Despite my own talents as a telepath, I wasn't able yet to clearly pluck their thoughts from the air, as was Kipp.

"They have targeted this stage.... but not because of us. They think there is a gold box on board."

I laughed softly. "Well, it seems that Steve Hill's

warning to the clerk at the stage company worked. They aren't after us, thinking I have a lot of money."

Pete's voice drifted back to me.

"Mrs. Totheroh, we're being forced to stop. You just stay inside and be quiet; let me handle this."

I was perfectly content to do just that and sat back on the bench, which was padded but not sufficiently to stave off hind end fatigue. I looked at Kipp whose eyes narrowed.

"My butt is sore, too," he commented. "I'm grateful to not be saddled, literally, with a bustle."

The rocking motion gently subsided, and had we been in an automobile, I would have been listening for a tiny squeal of brakes to accompany the stop. Instead, all I heard was the jangling of harness bits and the stomp of an equine foot.

"Driver, you know what we want, so you can go ahead and toss it down." There was a pause before the unfamiliar, gravelly voice added, "And tell your boy to put aside his shotgun."

Dave's thoughts were agitated and combative since he wanted to bring a fight to the robbers. But he succumbed to Pete's instructions, and I heard the clatter of the coach gun as it hit the wooden planks of the box. The sound of Pete's spitting was loud in the quiet desert air, and I saw the missile as it passed by my window. The sweet smell of tobacco wafted past my sensitive nose.

The bandits were careful to not use names, but I realized that they recognized Pete from past times they had encountered him as a driver. He had, occasionally, waged a battle when carrying Wells Fargo gold boxes, since he was being well compensated to make a delivery unsullied. I, of course, had given him the opposite instructions: don't fight and let's survive the trip to Tombstone.

A shadow fell across my window as a horse drew close. I saw a large brown eye and caught a whiff of hot, sweaty horse. Pushing my spine against the thinly padded seat, I hoped for invisibility. I glanced at Kipp; his eyes were rounded with the thrill of the moment, and his large mouth dropped open in a pant. Well, he'd wanted excitement, and we were slap dab in the middle of it.

I could see the rider as he dismounted; he cautiously approached Pete and Dave, watching them for any movement signaling an aggressive response. With a whistle he signaled another rider, who apparently approached from the rear of the coach to examine the boot. His efforts would lead to disappointment, since all that it contained was my small trunk and carpetbag. The robbers, with one another, were using names of reference in their minds, although they carefully avoided verbalizing them. Kipp's head darted up as he heard one of the men thinking 'Frank'.

"Could that be Frank Stillwell?" Kipp asked me.

I shrugged my shoulders.

"So what're you carrying?" the man's voice echoed out. The desert, with the lack of trees and shrubs, was a perfect void with no inanimate objects to disrupt sound waves.

"I've got a passenger today," Pete responded. "Just a lady," he added, "and I'd be grateful if you'd leave her alone." I knew that Pete kept a pistol concealed beneath the jacket he wore and could see his hand moving towards the gun. Despite what I'd told him, he was not going to let the highwaymen disturb me, if he could prevent it. It was quaintly chivalrous and totally unnecessary.

It was then that I felt the touch of a symbiotic mind weaving its way through the wooden walls of the coach. My eyes opened wide, and I stared at Kipp, whose head lifted in surprise. It was obvious one of the robbers holding us at bay was a fellow symbiont.

Over my four hundred plus years, I'd shared many memorable moments with my own species and recognized the existence of good and evil did not just reside with homosapiens. I'd recently experienced the intrusion of Andrea Collins into my mind by use of a method that was thoroughly discouraged by our group. It was subtle, to be sure, but still an unwelcomed event. But nothing in my past prepared me for what was about to happen.

A forceful telepathic mind began an investigation of me that pushed past the normal and acceptable boundaries and began to shred its way into the hidden rooms that I concealed from all, save Kipp. I desperately tried to close off my mind, but it was immediately clear that the other symbiont was more powerful than I, and I quickly lost ground to his assault. And yes, it was an assault, with no quantitative difference from a human physical attack in that it was equally intimate and horrifying. I gasped and clutched with my fists at the empty air; my eyes seemed to lose their normal vision, and I heard myself whimper softly.

Suddenly, Kipp was there, teeth bared in outraged fury. Over the relatively short time I'd been associated with him, there had been moments when he displayed gifts of our species that had been lost over centuries due to the consequences of a limited gene pool. But Kipp, fresh from the ancient world, was the genuine article, functioning as God had intended.

Kipp hopped over to my side of the small coach interior and began licking my face in a frantic attempt to gain my attention away from the unknown attacker. In my thoughts, I could hear Kipp growl again, fearsome and powerful. I don't know how he did it, but he pushed outward with his mind and slammed a door that effectively closed off the unwanted intrusion of the stranger. Kipp and I both recognized a burst of surprise followed by a wry mental chuckle. The other recognized Kipp's impressive talents and respected them.

I leaned forward and rested my sweat covered forehead on Kipp's furry pelt. He pushed his head to the window and narrowed his eyes as he looked off to the southwest where a lone man sat upon a horse, silhouetted by the late afternoon sun. The man—no, make that a male, humanoid symbiont—turned his head slightly and watched Kipp. A hand drew up and touched the brim of a hat in a sardonic salute. Something akin to envy crossed the yards between us and both Kipp and I realized that he had no symbiotic partner... at least not any more. I started to tell Kipp that he should not impulsively protect me before he turned to stare at me and uttered a quiet "shut up" command.

"I'm blocking him for now so don't distract me," Kipp finally commented. He resumed his attitude at the window. The lone figure finally gave voice to his humanoid companions.

"Boys, let's go. There's nothing to be had here."

The man who was in closest proximity to me was visibly irritated since he was looking forward to stealing any jewelry or money I might have. But there was a fear of the lone man and the name given to him in the minds of the others was 'Johnny'.

I looked at Kipp and he glanced back, once. If the symbiont was, indeed, Johnny Ringo, then he was notorious as a cold blooded killer of such an unpredictable temperament as to strike fear in the hearts of those he thought of as friends. Per history, even Curly Bill was wary of John Ringo.

If this were true, I wondered how one of my kind could evolve into such an antisocial monster? Kipp relaxed his vigilance when he felt the other symbiont pull back from his aggressive examination of me. As the man spurred his horse in retreat, a parting thought came our way.

"I'll see you both in Tombstone," the man said.

———◆———

TOMBSTONE, 1881
available in print and ebook

T.L.B. Wood began her appreciation of literature at an early age, encouraged by her mother who was an English teacher. T.L. is a certified adult behavioral health clinical nurse specialist and works as a case manager as well as a clinical instructor at a school of nursing. She and her husband share a love of nature, and more than one rescued dog or cat in need of a caring family has found a forever home with the Wood Family. When not feeding and caring for her menagerie, T.L. can be found at her desk, writing, or taking long walks as she envisioned new stories to be told.

You can contact T.L. through her publisher at
TLBWood@epublishingworks.com

www.ingramcontent.com/pod-product-compliance
Lightning Source LLC
Chambersburg PA
CBHW022145240626
47153CB00007B/2517